They walked back to the stairs, and Nick stopped before climbing. He placed the bin on the bottom step and turned to face Brynn. She held another container, one labeled *unisex clothes*, as if she'd been anticipating what might come next. He took that tub from her and put it on the cement floor.

"What do you want to happen?" He used one finger to tip her chin toward him when she looked away. "Tell me, Brynn, and I swear I'll do everything in my power to make it come to pass. Anything."

There was a second of vulnerability that flashed in her gaze, like she might truly let him in to help. As if he might finally get a chance to make up for some of the mistakes he'd made in the past. He'd do anything for that chance.

Then she blinked and her gaze shuttered. She elbowed him out of the way and hefted the bin he'd left on the step into her arms. "I want what's best for Tyler and for the baby. It's all that matters."

* * *

WELCOME TO STARLIGHT:
They swore they'd never fall in love...
but promises were made to be broken!

Dear Reader,

Welcome to Christmas in Starlight. I love the holiday season, filled with a special kind of magic and a little extra hope. Starlight native and single mom Brynn Hale needs all the hope she can get as she works to make a life for her son. But when a new baby comes into her life, there's only one man she can turn to for help, the one who long ago broke her heart. Brynn will need more than a Christmas miracle for a second chance at love.

Police chief Nick Dunlap never got over Brynn or the guilt from the pain he caused her when they were younger. He's vowed to keep his distance, but when she needs his help, Nick struggles to remember why he should avoid her. And the more they're together, the more his heart is unable to resist the connection. With some trust and a bit of Christmas magic, these two might be able to find their way back to each other again.

I hope you have a wonderful holiday season and would love to hear from you at www.michellemajor.com.

Big hugs,

Michelle

His Last-Chance Christmas Family

MICHELLE MAJOR

H HARLEQUIN

SPECIAL
EDITION

**HARLEQUIN®
SPECIAL
EDITION™**

Recycling programs
for this product may
not exist in your area.

ISBN-13: 978-1-335-89496-0

His Last-Chance Christmas Family

Copyright © 2020 by Michelle Major

All rights reserved. No part of this book may be used or reproduced in any manner whatsoever without written permission except in the case of brief quotations embodied in critical articles and reviews.

This is a work of fiction. Names, characters, places and incidents are either the product of the author's imagination or are used fictitiously. Any resemblance to actual persons, living or dead, businesses, companies, events or locales is entirely coincidental.

This edition published by arrangement with Harlequin Books S.A.

For questions and comments about the quality of this book, please contact us at CustomerService@Harlequin.com.

Harlequin Enterprises ULC
22 Adelaide St. West, 40th Floor
Toronto, Ontario M5H 4E3, Canada
www.Harlequin.com

Printed in U.S.A.

Michelle Major grew up in Ohio but dreamed of living in the mountains. Soon after graduating with a degree in journalism, she pointed her car west and settled in Colorado. Her life and house are filled with one great husband, two beautiful kids, a few furry pets and several well-behaved reptiles. She's grateful to have found her passion writing stories with happy endings. Michelle loves to hear from her readers at michellemajor.com.

Books by Michelle Major

Harlequin Special Edition

Welcome to Starlight

The Best Intentions
The Last Man She Expected

Crimson, Colorado

Anything for His Baby
A Baby and a Betrothal
Always the Best Man
Christmas on Crimson Mountain
Romancing the Wallflower
Sleigh Bells in Crimson
Coming Home to Crimson

The Fortunes of Texas: Rambling Rose

Fortune's Fresh Start

The Fortunes of Texas: The Secret Fortunes

A Fortune in Waiting

Visit the Author Profile page
at Harlequin.com for more titles.

To the Special Edition team.
Thank you for making my books shine.

Chapter One

Brynn Hale glanced at her watch, fifteen minutes late for her lunch date. She checked her cell phone, which still displayed *No Service* in the top left corner of the screen.

Another turn of the key in the car's ignition produced only a hollow click, click, click.

She muttered a curse under her breath and immediately felt guilty. Her mother had taught her from a young age that swearing was unladylike. While Brynn had disappointed her mom in so many ways, at least she kept her language clean. Usually.

Desperate times and all that.

In the distance, she heard the sound of a car

engine, a first since she'd realized her old Toyota sedan wouldn't start on this lonely stretch of mountain highway.

She climbed out of the car, which she'd parked on the shoulder near the sharp curve of Devil's Landing, into the cool mountain air. The location was only about twenty minutes outside the town limits of Starlight, Washington, where she'd lived for her entire twenty-eight years.

It hadn't been her plan to become a townie. Most everything about Brynn's current life hadn't been part of how she'd dreamed things would turn out.

She'd made the best of things, even the events that had rocked her to her core, which was what had prompted her visit to mile marker six on this cold, damp December day.

Easing around her car, she was careful to stay to one side of the white line that bordered the two-lane highway. A lift into town would be good, a trip to the ER because she got herself hit by a passing motorist not so much.

Her stomach dipped as she realized the approaching SUV had police lights on the roof. Not Nick. Let it be anyone but Starlight's police chief.

The urge to return to her car and duck was almost overwhelming, but it wouldn't do any good. The officer was bound to stop. She lifted her arms to wave just as her boot heel caught on a random patch of ice. She lost her balance, dropping to one knee before righting herself.

"Son of a biscuit," she said through clenched teeth. The fall had ripped a hole in her new black tights and tiny pieces of gravel stuck to her palms.

Before she had time to brush them off, the police vehicle had lurched to a stop next to her car, blue and red lights suddenly flashing, beacons of color against the dreary gray of the winter day.

Because that's how her day was going, Nick Dunlap bolted from the car and rushed toward her.

"Brynn, are you okay?"

Her breath caught in her throat as he reached for her, grabbing her wrists and examining her hands before giving her an intense once-over. His honey-brown eyes were filled with worry—panic if she was reading him correctly. The smell of cinnamon gum and spice drifted over her, a potent mix she always associated with Nick.

Brynn hated the flood of memories that scent evoked.

"What's wrong?" he demanded. "Are you hurt? Tell me."

She yanked away from him, frustrated at her visceral reaction to the warmth of his calloused hands on her skin. "What's wrong with you?" she countered. "You're being overdramatic."

"Overdramatic," he repeated, taking a step back, the mask of stalwart police chief falling over his handsome features. Nick had always been too good-looking, with thick hair, chiseled features, an easy grin that showcased the most annoyingly adorable dimples Brynn had ever seen on a person.

He'd been a girl magnet since his family moved to town in third grade, first on the Starlight Elementary playground and then in the hallways of the high school, at the local football field, and behind the bleachers and too many places for Brynn to count. Places she'd never experienced with him.

The most popular boy in school didn't take his best friend and sidekick behind the bleachers. Nick spent time with Brynn in the library and in his mother's cozy kitchen and watching reruns or playing video games in the family's remodeled basement.

Brynn had been the literal girl next door, even though she'd always wanted more from Nick. Things he couldn't—or wouldn't—offer her. Always, until those few minutes peeing on a stick in her pink bathroom just before high school graduation had changed everything.

"Do you know where you are?" he asked, turning his gaze to the valley below them. Their town was down there, under the fog that clung to the mountain today.

She felt her jaw clench. "Of course I know."

"And the date?"

"Yes," she whispered.

"Then why the hell are you here?"

"None of your business."

He scrubbed a hand over his face. "Tell me anyway," he said, his voice calmer. Low and gentle. The little hairs on the back of her neck stood on end. "Please," he added, which was a nice touch. "Because I've got all kinds of bizarre rationales running through my mind at the moment."

"What kind of rationales?"

His gaze flicked to the section of guardrail that was newer than the rest, rebuilt after her late husband's truck had slammed into it before hurtling off the side of the cliff and landing in a fiery crash two hundred feet below.

"Do you think I came out here to follow Daniel into the great beyond?" In the list of life moments that made Brynn feel like swearing a blue streak, this one vaulted to the top. "Are you joking?"

She paced to the edge of the barricade and then back again, hands fisted at her sides, anger and disbelief flooding through her.

"I thought you knew me," she told him tightly.

He blew out a breath. "I do."

"I would never…" She closed her eyes, mentally counted to ten. "I have Tyler to think of. You know that." Her ten-year-old son was everything to her. Even the suggestion that she might risk the chance to raise him, especially from someone like Nick, cut her to the core.

"I know. Brynn, I'm sorry. Seeing you out here on this day and then watching you fall to your knees...it caught me off guard." The emotion in his voice did funny things to her insides. Then he placed a hand on her arm, and she had to force herself not to shift away from him again. "Tell me why you're here."

She looked down, noticing for the first time a tiny spot of blood on her knee where the tights had ripped. "I have a date."

Nick went completely still in front of her, so she continued, "Mara set me up with a guy from Weatherby who came into the coffee shop last week when he drove over on business." Her friend Mara Johnson managed Main Street Perk, Starlight's popular local coffee joint. "I wanted to tell Daniel, and it felt strange to go to his grave site. This was the last place he was alive, so I came here."

"A date?"

Brynn glanced up at Nick, who was now looking at her like she'd sprouted a second head. Although he normally kept his sandy blond hair cut short, it was in need of a trim and a thick lock fell over his forehead. He had broad shoulders and a muscled build that filled out his dark police uniform in a way that would have most women begging him to handcuff them.

Not Brynn.

She wouldn't ask Nick Dunlap for a single thing

if she had any choice in the matter. "You keep repeating what I say," she pointed out.

"I'm trying to process this and also get my heart to slow down. Seriously, you scared the hell out of me."

"I'm not yours to worry about," she reminded him.

A muscle ticked in his jaw. "Duly noted, but friends show concern for each other."

Friends, she thought to herself, trying not to let him see what that word did to her. Brynn and Nick could tell everyone they were friends. But it wasn't like it had been before. She missed those easy days.

He released her arm. "I thought you'd decided against dating."

She crossed her arms over her chest as a brisk gust of air blew up from the valley, whispering through the pine trees that surrounded them. "Can you give me a ride into town, Chief? I'm already late."

"What about your car?"

"It's the alternator. Jimmy warned me it needed to be replaced the last time I had the car into his shop for an oil change, but I never got around to it. Now I will."

"You can't ignore stuff like that."

"Nick, come on. Save the lecture and just give me a ride. I'll call Jimmy after lunch and have him send a tow truck for the car."

"I could take a look at it," he offered.

"Not your problem."

He looked like he wanted to argue but gave a small nod instead. "Grab whatever you need and make sure it's locked."

"Thanks." She turned for the Toyota, then spun back around. "Hey, Nick?"

One side of his mouth curved. "Yeah?"

"What were you doing up here today?"

He shrugged. "It's the five-month anniversary of Daniel's death. Same as you, in a way, minus the dating part. I was visiting my buddy."

"Oh." Emotion tumbled through her like debris coming down the side of a hill after a rockslide. The reminder that Nick was her late husband's friend as much as hers shouldn't hurt her at this point.

But it did.

"Tell me more about dating," Nick said, relieved his voice didn't waver as he made the request. He would never admit how much the thought of Brynn in another man's arms affected him. Hell, he'd been one of the groomsmen in her quickie wedding to Daniel Hale a decade ago and had managed to stay friendly with both of them over the ensuing years.

He'd blown his chance with Brynn back in high school, when he'd been a selfish, egotistical, immature kid. Maybe he'd grown up a little since that time, but he knew he still didn't deserve a woman like her.

Not that Daniel had, either. When he'd told her he'd driven up to Devil's Landing, the picturesque overlook in the hills to the east of town, because of the anniversary of Daniel's death, it hadn't been a lie. But he wasn't there to honor a friend. Nick had so much pent-up anger over the way Daniel had treated Brynn during their marriage, carelessly like she was some sort of old pair of shoes instead of his precious wife.

Whatever friendship he'd had with Daniel had been cut short by the other man's callous actions, the serial cheating and constant disrespect. After the accident, Nick's anger mixed with guilt, an almost untenable brew. What if he had pushed Daniel to give up the women? What if he'd convinced him to try to make his marriage work?

What if Nick had asked Brynn not to marry Daniel in the first place?

He hadn't done any of those things. He'd minded his own business and kept both Daniel and Brynn at a friendly arm's length. Driving through the winding roads of the Cascades' towering pine forests with Brynn next to him somehow calmed Nick. He needed all the calm he could muster to handle what was coming next.

"It's fairly straightforward," Brynn replied, and he noticed the edge in her tone. She tucked a lock of dark hair behind one delicate ear. Everything about Brynn was delicate. Her small frame, pale skin and clear blue eyes framed by thick dark lashes. She looked more like a fairy-tale princess who should be conversing with tiny forest creatures than the overworked single mom she was. "I'm meeting a guy for lunch. Maybe we'll hit it off. If not—"

"The last I heard, you wanted nothing to do with dating. You were devoted to Tyler."

He heard her soft gasp and realized he'd said the wrong thing. Nothing new where Brynn was concerned, he supposed.

"I mean—"

"I understand what you mean." One finger picked at the edge of the hole in the fabric above her knee. "Mara and Kaitlin are convinced it will be good for me." She turned to him. "Going out to lunch with a stranger has nothing to do with my devotion to my son."

"I know. I'm sorry. Really sorry." His fingers tightened around the steering wheel. "I'm still not thinking clearly. You're a great mom. The best. No one compares. If there was an award for—"

"Nick, stop."

He blew out a relieved breath when she laughed. The last thing he wanted to do was hurt Brynn. She'd been through enough already.

"I did say at Mara and Parker's wedding that I wasn't interested in dating, and I'm still not sure I'm doing the right thing. Maybe this is too soon, but it's no secret my marriage wasn't exactly a happy one."

They'd gotten to town and he turned to her at the traffic light at Starlight's main intersection. "You deserve to be happy."

Her lips curved into a genuine smile, and it made his heart sing at the same time his chest squeezed painfully. He didn't want to consider Brynn happy with another man.

"Can you drop me at The Diner?" she asked after a long moment.

The Diner was a popular place in Starlight, one that was sure to have lots of locals happy to gossip about the widow out with a new man.

"Sure." He drummed his fingers on the console between the two seats, trying to appear like he didn't want to follow the man she was meeting out of the restaurant and find some flimsy excuse to pull him over and harass him for the heck of it. Nick wouldn't do that. His personal life might not be much to speak of, but he prided himself on being a good cop and leader for his town.

It had taken a tragedy for him to wise up and make something of himself, but he'd done it. And he had more sense than to mess it up now.

"Mara and Kaitlin are calling their little project the twelve dates of Christmas. They have a whole list of potential men to match me with until I find the right one."

He swallowed back the bile that rose to his throat. "You're going on dates with twelve different guys?"

"Hopefully not. I can barely find time to brush my teeth some days. Wait a minute. Are you slut shaming me, Nick Dunlap?" She unclicked her seat belt as he pulled to the curb in front of the restaurant. "I know you." She wagged a finger in his direction. "Not just Chief Dunlap. I knew Tricky Nicky and your revolving door of girlfriends from high school. You might remember it was my house you sneaked over to the night that half the cheerleading squad showed up on your front lawn so you could vote on which one was the hottest."

He pressed two fingers against the side of his temples. "God, I was an ass."

"You still are from the sound of it."

He almost laughed at the truth in her statement. That was the problem with Brynn, or with his reaction to Brynn. He wanted to be her friend and support her but always managed to say the wrong thing. She was right. She did know him—or at least had known him—better than anyone. He hadn't been alone with her, even for something as straightforward as a car ride, since high school.

It had been easy enough to put her in the category of "might have been" when she was married to Daniel. Nick had locked up any feelings he had for her that went beyond friendship. Up until recently, he'd believed the key to that lock had been thrown away along with so many other childhood dreams.

But now…

He shook his head. No. Daniel's death didn't change anything. Nick knew he wasn't cut out for love. After hurting Brynn once, he wouldn't take the chance of doing it again.

"I want you to be happy," he said again. "I hope this date, and any of your other twelve-men-a-milking or pear-tree-partridge outings go well. Seriously, I do."

"No partridges or milking men," she said with another small laugh. "It's lunch. Not a big deal."

Tell that to his heart.

"If you need anything, or if Tyler needs anything…" He cleared his throat. "Just know I'm still your friend."

Her gaze gentled. Brynn was far stronger than she looked, stronger than most people gave her credit for, including him for too long.

She'd gotten married at eighteen to a boy she barely knew after their first sexual encounter left her pregnant. Ten years later, her husband died in a car crash, but he hadn't been alone in the truck when it careened off that cliff. His mistress had been in the passenger seat, and in a small town like Starlight, that fact was big news.

But he'd never seen Brynn cower from the gossip or do anything but hold her head high and keep moving forward. He guessed her motivation came from Tyler and her desire to be a role model for her son. Either way, he admired her quiet strength.

"That goes both ways," she said quietly. "I know the holidays can be rough for you."

He scoffed even as his gut tightened. "I'm fine. Busy at the station, which is how I like it. December is like any other month to me."

She studied him for a long moment, and his inclination was to fidget like a naughty schoolboy caught with his hand in the cookie jar. But he managed to keep his expression neutral.

"Will you be at the tree lighting tonight?"

"On duty," he confirmed. Every year, the residents of Starlight kicked off the holiday season in front of town hall with the annual lighting of the town's Christmas tree. The women's auxiliary would serve hot cocoa and the local choir led everyone in singing carols to celebrate the countdown to Christmas.

Nick always volunteered to work the event because so many of his deputies had families to attend with. He had…well, his mom. What self-respecting late-twenties bachelor would admit that fact?

"I'll see you there," she said with a final smile.

"You can tell me how your date went," he responded.

Her eyebrows shot up in response, but she nodded. "Sure, Nick. What a funny role reversal for us. Me sharing my dating adventures instead of the other way around."

"Good luck."

He didn't move for almost a full minute after she disappeared into the cheery restaurant. *Funny* was the last word he'd use to describe the thought of listening to Brynn's stories of dating other men.

Friendship. That was all Nick had to offer, he reminded himself. He'd been a lousy friend when they were younger and distant since her marriage. He had a chance to make up for that now. It was December, the month of increased caring and generosity, and he was going to make sure Brynn's Christmas was a merry one.

Chapter Two

Brynn held Tyler's small hand later that night as she scanned the crowd that had already gathered in front of town hall. She'd parked a few blocks away and owed a debt of thanks to Nick. When she'd called Jimmy at the auto shop after the most boring lunch date in the history of the world, he'd informed her Nick had already been by about her car.

According to Jimmy, the chief had insisted that towing Brynn's car needed to be moved to the top of the shop's priority list. They'd dispatched a truck, brought in the vehicle and installed the new alternator.

All Brynn needed to do was bring in her keys

so they could make sure there were no other issues and she'd be all set.

Nick's unexpected thoughtfulness had saved her an entire afternoon, additional time off work and the headache of dealing with the repair. She'd gotten used to handling life's little crises on her own since Daniel's accident, but that didn't mean she liked it. The sense of relief and gratitude at having someone take care of a problem so she didn't have to overwhelmed her. The fact that Nick had been the one to come to her rescue made her stomach flutter in a way she hadn't anticipated.

Brynn had long ago given up her childhood crush on Nick Dunlap. Nothing dampened teenage ardor like a blatant rejection that led to a surprise pregnancy with the boy she'd chosen as her "rebound." Having sex—her first time—with Daniel Hale had possibly been the most spontaneous and rash decision Brynn had ever made in her life.

Lesson learned.

Tyler squeezed her fingers, reminding her that despite the broken promises and unfulfilled dreams she'd endured as a result of those few minutes, it had all been worth it.

"I see Logan and Jake," he told her. He pointed to two boys weaving through the crowd. "Can I go say hi?"

She let go of his hand. "Sure, sweetie, but…"

Tyler didn't wait for her to finish. He dashed toward his friends with all the confidence of a kid who'd been attending the annual holiday event every December he could remember.

"Find me for the lighting," she finished, then bit down on the inside of her cheek. Her son was still young but growing up every day, becoming more independent and sometimes a little sassy. The sass had ramped up a notch since his father's death. The adjustment from being a mother to filling all the parental duties tried the patience of both Brynn and Tyler. Daniel hadn't been the world's best dad, but he'd loved his son. Tyler clearly felt his absence in ways that made him lash out at the one person who would tolerate the emotional roller coaster he often seemed to be riding.

They'd always attended the tree lighting as a family. Most years, Daniel would head to the bar with buddies from work after, but they'd be together as a unit for the ceremony. Tyler loved to perch on his father's shoulders, and the happiness in her son's eyes had made Brynn's heart glad. It had made everything that was wrong with her marriage seem not so important.

Now she was alone. Sure, she had Tyler and told Mara and Kaitlin he was enough. He filled her heart, but she knew she needed more in her life. For Tyler's benefit if no other reason. Brynn had been raised by a single mom and always understood the sacrifices her mother made to raise her.

Her mom had wanted more for Brynn, and Brynn had disappointed her in the most fundamental way possible. She never wanted Tyler to feel like he was a burden or responsible for his mother's happiness. Brynn had to manage that on her own.

"Are you going to join everyone or watch from back here?"

She turned to find Nick standing behind her, still in his dark police uniform, but now with the addition of a canvas jacket to ward off the cold. At six foot three, he towered over her, as he'd done since he hit puberty at the end of seventh grade and shot up seven inches before they got to high school.

Fighting against her innate physical awareness of him, Brynn shrugged. "I'm girding my loins, as the saying goes."

He grimaced. "That always sounded painful to me."

She laughed despite the nerves running through her. "It's our first Christmas without Daniel," she said, suddenly sober.

"Yep." He shifted closer. "You okay?"

The question felt different than when he'd huffed out the words at her on the side of the road. Or she felt different. Not so revved up with anger and bitterness. The start of the holiday season made her wistful, so much potential for kindness and cheer. Over the years, life had given her ample reasons to believe more in the stresses of the season—loneliness, missed opportunities, unrealistic expectations.

But December always gave her hope for something better.

This year she wasn't sure how she felt. *Okay* didn't seem to come anywhere close.

"I want to make the season special for Tyler. Even though they seemed silly at the time, we had traditions that involved his father. Putting up the tree with Daniel cursing a blue streak. The cat knocking ornaments to the floor after it was decorated, which led to more cursing. Pancakes on Christmas morning—"

"Tell me those didn't involve cursing," Nick said with a sigh.

"Not usually." She smiled even as her throat grew tight with the emotion balled there. "Our life wasn't perfect, but it's what Tyler knew. I don't know how to be both Mom and Dad for him. I want him to be happy. I want to be happy, but it's been a long time since I'd describe myself that way. I'm not sure if I know how to get back there." Her voice cracked, and she didn't bother to hide it. She and Nick might not be close any longer, but he was still her first best friend.

The relief that washed over her at not having to pretend to be fine was a shock, but she leaned into it nonetheless, allowing herself to feel everything she'd tamped down for the past five months.

Nick ran a hand through his hair, looking ten kinds of uncomfortable at her confession. "You'll figure it out."

"Definitely don't quit your day job to become a therapist," she advised with an eye roll and an elbow nudge to his ribs.

Nick chuckled, then asked, "Did the date today make you happy?"

"Did you know tapeworms don't have a stomach, so they absorb nutrients from the outside in?"

"Um...no." He turned to her more fully. "Tell me that wasn't part of your conversation over lunch."

"Not just part," she clarified. "Turns out Mara's partridge in a pear tree is a scientist who researches parasites. He teaches at Gonzaga and was on his way to a conference in Seattle when he passed through Starlight last week."

"No wonder he needed to be set up on a blind date. With those kind of skills, he's probably in the longest dating dry spell known to man."

"Ouch," she whispered. "What does it say about me that I needed to be set up?"

His hazel eyes were intense on her. "Your situation is different."

"Right." She threw up her hands. "The poor grieving widow and single mom. Textbook pathetic."

"No one thinks you're pathetic."

"They feel sorry for me," she countered. "Which

might be as bad. It's why you found me standing back here. My circumstances make people uncomfortable."

"Don't say that."

His voice skimmed over her like a cool breeze on a summer day. There was a reason she'd kept her distance from Nick. Her physical reaction to him had been a constant in her life and seemingly out of her control, as if her body came to life when he was around. She should walk away but couldn't— wouldn't was more like it. She'd spent most of her life shifting away from difficulties, glossing over trouble with a smile on her face. Always the good girl, always the person who could be relied on to put those around her at ease.

Where had it gotten her?

No place she'd recommend that anyone visit.

Since Daniel's death, Brynn had begun to change. The parts of her she recognized were quickly disappearing to be replaced with pieces that felt raw and rough. It started at the funeral, where she'd sat in the first pew of the church and fought the urge to scream at the top of her lungs. To shout at her dead husband for the reckless, hurtful choices he'd made and at herself for becoming so small it felt like her entire existence could fit on the sharp tip of a thumbtack.

There had been no outburst, of course. She'd remained calm and composed for her son, who quietly cried next to her. She'd cried for him and for the hand life had dealt her. Then a few days later, when he'd gone back to school, she'd driven up to Devil's Landing, the same stretch of road where Nick had found her today. She'd gotten out of her car, walked to the edge, where bright orange cones and caution tape marked the spot of Daniel's accident.

There, she'd screamed and screamed until her throat burned and her voice gave out. It had been such a relief to release the sound, her wails echoing across the valley.

That moment had freed something in Brynn, and she'd spent the past five months recalibrating her internal life to try to honor the change. It felt monumental. So she wouldn't—couldn't—walk away from a difficult conversation or her latent feelings for Nick. Not anymore.

"I make you uncomfortable," she told him, the words stated as fact rather than opinion.

"No." The denial fell flat, and he blew out a long breath. "I'm your friend, Brynn. I want to be your friend again. I'm simply not sure how to do it anymore. God knows I made a mess of things the first time."

"You did," she agreed, and his eyes widened. "Did I shock you?"

His broad shoulders lifted, then lowered. "A little. You never used to call me out on any of the crap I pulled."

"I'm not the same as I used to be."

"I'm glad."

This time it was her turn for shock. "You used to count on me being your mealymouthed sidekick."

"If I treated you that way, I'm sorry. It's good to know you're taking a stand for yourself." He lifted a hand, as if to reach for her, then lowered it again. *Yes*, her traitorous body screamed. *Please touch me. No*, her mind admonished. *That's a terrible idea.* "I've grown up, too."

Brynn didn't want to notice all the ways Nick had grown up. He'd been boyishly handsome as a teen, all rangy limbs and lean muscles, but had indeed developed into more.

"I should join everyone before they start the ceremony," she told him, needing some space from the rush of emotion this quiet moment with him had unleashed inside her.

He nodded. "I'm going to check around back."

"Do high school students still drink in the shadows behind town hall?" she asked with a smile.

"Some things change in Starlight," he answered. "Some things stay the same."

She thunked the heel of her palm against her forehead. "Oh, my gosh. I almost forgot to thank you for taking care of my car. You didn't need to do that, Nick."

"Not a big deal. Jimmy has a habit of getting rowdy when he's drinking. He owes me for all the rides home from the bar before he could get himself into trouble."

Her instinct was to protest again or make a statement about how she could have handled the car on her own. She didn't like to rely on anyone. Pretty much everyone in town knew her circumstances. The only way she was able to hold her head high was by making it seem like she could take care of anything. But this was Nick, and she didn't have to pretend. "It was a huge help, and I appreciate it."

The look of satisfaction that crossed his face made her breath catch in her throat.

"You're welcome," he told her, and with a final wave, she hurried to join the crowd in front of town hall.

Too much time with Nick wouldn't help her to feel more in control of things.

She caught sight of Tyler at the hot cocoa stand, and he grinned as he held up a handful of marshmallows, then popped the whole bunch into his mouth.

The laugh that escaped her lips felt refreshingly normal. Normal was a balm to her battered soul these days, and she loved seeing her son enjoying the event without the weight of memories she couldn't seem to shake off.

"You're here. We've been looking for you."

She turned toward Kaitlin Carmody and Mara Johnson, her two closest friends in Starlight. Neither of them were natives to the small town, which

Brynn guessed was part of what made her so comfortable with them. Yes, they knew her situation, but there was none of the complicated judgment from either of them that seemed to define most of her longtime friendships in the community.

They both had regrets from their own pasts, and the acceptance they gave her had immediately put her at ease. No preconceived notions of who she was supposed to be or all the ways she hadn't lived up to her potential as she'd tried to make her marriage work and raise her son in a loving home.

Since Daniel died, they'd gotten even closer, and she couldn't imagine life without them.

"I'm so happy you're both here." She hugged each of the women and made certain a smile was fixed on her face. Honesty with Nick was one thing, but she wasn't about to let her tumbling emotions put a damper on the start of the holiday season for Kaitlin and Mara.

"Finn, Parker and Josh are saving a spot near the front so the kids will have an unobstructed view of the tree," Kaitlin told her.

"That's sweet," Brynn murmured. Although she'd been closer with Nick, she'd also been friends with Finn Samuelson and Parker Johnson most of her life. Josh was Parker's younger brother, and his daughter, Anna, had become besties with Mara's little girl, Evie, when Mara moved to Starlight over a year ago. "Tyler is with his buddies right now, so

I need to round him up." She checked her watch. "We have a few minutes before the ceremony is scheduled to start. Why are the two of you looking at me like that?"

"The date," Mara said, pushing a thick strand of bourbon-colored hair behind her ear. "You haven't said anything."

Brynn shrugged. "He's into tapeworms."

"That's not a thing." Kaitlin grimaced. "Tell me that's not a thing."

"It's part of the science curriculum he teaches," Brynn explained. "And he's kind of obsessed. Parasites don't do it for me, so I'm not sure we're a good match."

Her friends stared wide-eyed a moment longer, then both of them dissolved into fits of laughter.

"Gross," Mara said, shaking her head.

"You should add *no parasites* to your online dating profile," Kaitlin advised.

"I don't have a profile," Brynn reminded her. "If you'll remember, I think this whole dating thing is a waste of time."

Kaitlin grew serious as she touched the diamond engagement ring that graced the third finger of her left hand. "Love is never a waste of time."

"She's right," Mara confirmed. "And sometimes you find it in the unlikeliest place. You can't give up. We're committed to this quest."

Brynn's cheeks ached with the effort of keeping

her smile steady. She appreciated her friends and had been glad to watch them find love in Starlight. First Kaitlin with Finn and then Mara and Parker, an unlikely match in so many ways, particularly because he'd represented Mara's ex-husband in their divorce.

Both couples had overcome plenty of difficulties on the road to their happily-ever-after. Brynn wasn't convinced she was on the same path.

"Being set up makes me feel more like a charity case," she admitted.

"Don't say that." Mara reached for her hand, squeezing gently. "Everyone agrees you deserve a great man in your life."

"I have one in Tyler," she replied automatically.

"A man other than your son," Kaitlin clarified.

Brynn groaned. "When you put it like that, it sounds even more desperate than I feel."

"You aren't desperate. You're willing."

"Which makes it seem like I've scrawled my contact info on every bathroom stall this side of the Cascade Mountains."

"Don't be silly. Also, Finn met with the new owner of the hardware store yesterday. He came in to talk about an expansion loan. He's pretty cute and single."

Finn's family owned First Trust, the longest-running local bank in Starlight, since the institution's founding. Finn had returned to Starlight to help his ailing father with the bank this past summer, and although he and Kaitlin had started off more as enemies than friends, they'd quickly discovered love.

Brynn was happy for both of her friends and tried to ignore the sliver of envy that ran through her. "Did he put *single* on his application?" she asked with a raised brow. "Or did you interrogate him?"

Kaitlin headed up customer relations at the bank. The slim blonde sniffed. "*Interrogate* is such a harsh word. We talked and I mentioned I have a gorgeous friend who knows the best places to eat in Starlight."

"There are three restaurants in this town, if you don't count the food trucks at the mill." She nodded. "The food truck variety is awesome, if I do say so myself."

"Then you can take him on a date to the mill."

"I work there. That's weird." Brynn's pregnancy had changed so many things about her future. She'd planned to start her freshman year at Washington State University the fall after graduating high school, but instead had been dealing with swollen ankles and adjusting to marriage with a boy she barely knew. Over the years, she'd worked odd jobs around town, cleaning office buildings at night and doing filing for the local attorney and accountant's office—things that allowed her flexible hours so she didn't have to put her son in day care or rely on anyone to help.

No one had expected Brynn to handle motherhood well, so she'd been determined to prove everyone wrong. Once Tyler started elementary school, she'd worked in the front office and as a substitute teacher. She'd also volunteered for the PTO and in the classroom, her quest to demonstrate her worth never ending.

More recently, Parker and Josh Johnson had redeveloped the Dennison Mill, the town's deserted lumber mill, into a smorgasbord of adaptive-reuse space. There were retail stores, a second location for Main Street Perk, as well as community events. Somehow, Brynn had found the nerve to convince the brothers to hire her as their marketing and events manager. She'd planned to study advertising in college, and although she didn't have a degree, she loved the challenge of coming up with a plan for the mill.

"The mill is awesome," Mara said, "and so is your work there." She turned to Kaitlin. "What's number two's name anyway?"

"Number two?" Brynn questioned.

"Will MacFarlane," Kaitlin answered, then winked at Brynn. "Date number two of twelve."

"Oh, lord. That sounds bad."

"You're getting into the holiday spirit."

"I'm going to need heavy spirits to get through all these dates."

"Not if number two becomes your number one,"

Mara said with a cheeky grin. "Then you can have the rest of the dates with him. Mr. Right."

"I don't believe in Mr. Right," Brynn said, even as an image of Nick flitted across her mind.

"At least be open to Mr. Right Now," Mara urged. "We hung mistletoe at both locations of Perk."

Brynn stumbled a step as Tyler's thin arms wrapped around her legs. "Mom, I almost lost you."

"You didn't lose me, sweetie." She ruffled his hair. "I was waiting for you right here."

"I can't see the tree," he complained, craning his neck to see around the people who surrounded them. "I want to see."

Brynn's heart pinched, knowing that this year was different since her son wouldn't be higher than everyone else on his father's shoulders.

"Then let's go to where you can," Mara told him without missing a beat and led the way toward the front of the crowd.

"You'll have the best view ever," Brynn promised, taking his smaller hand in hers. As she followed her two friends, she vowed that no matter how hard she had to work, this Christmas was going to be the most magical she could make it.

Chapter Three

"Stop lying to yourself," Finn counseled a few nights later over a round of beers at Trophy Room, Starlight's most popular bar.

"And to Brynn," Parker added for good measure.

"Whose side are the two of you on?" Nick demanded, his voice pitched to almost a growl. He was sick of being lectured by his two closest friends. Drinking alone at home was starting to seem like a way better option.

"Hers," Parker said at the same time as Finn's emphatic, "Yours."

Finn immediately swatted Parker on the arm. "Dude."

"Both of yours."

"Said like a true attorney," Nick mumbled.

Parker flashed an unapologetic grin. "I take that as a compliment."

Nick grunted. "Don't." He held up a hand when Finn would have spoken again, took a moment to drain his beer, then returned the empty pilsner glass to the scuffed tabletop with a thud. "I've told you guys a hundred times now. Brynn and I are friends. Nothing more. Nothing less."

"Then you're going to lose her," Parker answered.

"Again," Finn added. "I don't understand why you're being so stubborn about this."

"I hurt her," Nick said as if it explained everything. "I won't take the chance of repeating that."

"You were an idiot." Finn grabbed a chip from the heaping pile of nachos in the middle of the table.

It was a Monday night, and a crowd had gathered in the bar's wood-paneled interior for food, drinks and football. The atmosphere was downright festive, even though neither of the teams playing tonight were located within a thousand miles of Washington State. Ever since he'd joined the force, Nick had gotten into the habit of assessing any space he entered, and he detected only camaraderie in the bar tonight.

"We all did plenty of stupid things back in high school," Parker added before digging into the nachos.

"Like the pact we made," Finn said.

Parker nodded as he shoved a loaded chip into his mouth. "Incredibly stupid."

"You only think that because you're in love." Nick didn't bother to hide the derision in his tone as he emphasized the final two words with air quotes.

"Don't air quote at me," Finn told him. "That vow was made out of fear and immaturity."

Parker nodded. "Apparently some of us haven't grown up."

Nick drew in a deep breath and forced himself not to push back from the table and stalk away from his friends. It annoyed the hell out of him that just because they'd both jumped on the truelove bandwagon he was automatically expected to hitch a ride.

He didn't need or want love in his life, no matter how his body reacted to Brynn. Maybe he couldn't control the beating of his heart, but he damn well had control over whether he gave it away.

Back in high school, Finn and Parker had felt the same. They'd all been hurting in different ways, but one thing the three of them had agreed on was that love wasn't worth the pain it could cause. The night of their high school graduation, after too many swigs of cheap liquor, they'd taken an oath not to fall in love. It might sound silly and they'd been more than a little drunk, but on that night, Finn, Parker and Nick had been serious about honoring the promise they made to each other.

Nick had woken up the next morning, his head pounding under the bright morning sun. Parker and

Finn had still been asleep a few feet from him, both of them snoring loud enough to rival a freight train. He'd felt sick and cotton-mouthed but his heart, for the first time since he'd seen Brynn dancing with Daniel Hale at prom, had been light.

The friends had rarely talked about that oath over the years. All of them had been eager to leave their hometown behind and set out to make their way in the world. Nick had been the first one to return when his mom's health declined after his brother's death in Afghanistan and the subsequent fatal heart attack his father suffered.

In Starlight, people settled down. Plenty of women he'd known growing up—and some new to town— had been interested in enticing him to settle down.

He'd never been the least bit tempted.

The vow, he'd told himself. It was because of the vow.

It had been a shock when Finn and then Parker had thrown aside their oath and fallen in love. He didn't want to resent them for their choices. Hell, Kaitlin and Mara were awesome.

But when Nick made a vow, he kept it. Even if he was the only one. Not that he'd had a reason to break the vow since that night, or a woman who made him want to give up on the promise he'd made.

"Nothing is going to happen between Brynn and me."

"Fine." Finn gave a disgusted sigh. "It's probably better anyway. She needs someone steady in her life. A man she can count on."

"I'm steady as a ro—" Nick clamped shut his mouth. Without a doubt, his friend was trying to bait him. He wouldn't fall for it.

"I met the new owner of the hardware supply company Kaitlin wants to introduce her to," Parker offered. "Seems like a decent guy. Maybe they'll hit it off."

"What's the damn obsession with finding Brynn a boyfriend?" Nick demanded. "Can't you keep your women occupied?"

Finn and Parker stared at him with twin expressions of horror on their faces. "You better not let Mara hear you talk like that," Parker warned.

"Kaitlin would skin you alive for that comment," Finn agreed.

"I know. I know." Nick held up his hands. "I realize I sound like an oaf. It's a new habit."

"*Oaf* is one word for it." Finn pushed the plate of nachos toward him.

"Need anything, fellas?" They all turned as Jordan Schaeffer, the former NFL tight end who'd moved to Starlight after a career-ending injury, approached the table. "Damn, Chief, you look like someone peed in your Wheaties."

"We're talking about the quest to find a guy for Brynn Hale," Finn explained. "It's making him grumpy as hell."

Nick sighed. "Do you really think she'd want us discussing her love life in the middle of a bar?"

"I know all about it." Jordan flipped a towel over one beefy shoulder. "Mara brought me a plate of cinnamon rolls the other day and asked what my idea of a perfect first date would be. Brynn is sure pretty and sweet as can be…"

Nick's gut clenched as he glared at Jordan.

"But not my type," Jordan finished quickly. "Another round?"

"No." Unable to endure this topic any longer, Nick straightened from his chair. "In case any of you are wondering, Brynn's perfect first date would be a hike in the woods, followed by a quiet dinner and watching some late-nineties rom-com to end the evening."

"Not that you're going to do anything with that bit of insider knowledge," Finn said, shaking his head.

"I'm going to go home and take Teddy for a walk." Nick thought of his dopey black Lab and smiled. "He's way better company than any of you."

A chorus of chuckles followed him away from the table, but he ignored his friends. It didn't matter what anyone thought he should do with Brynn. She was strictly relegated to the friend zone.

He walked out into the clear evening and took a breath so deep the cold air burned his lungs. He welcomed the pain, something to focus on other than the ache in his heart. Just as he got to his truck, a woman climbed out of a small hatchback parked behind him at the curb.

"Nick Dunlap?" she asked, voice trembling. "Are you Chief Dunlap?"

"Yes, ma'am." His law-enforcement spidey sense went on high alert. "How can I help you?"

The woman took a step closer and then glanced toward her vehicle. In the glow of the streetlight above it, Nick could see the outline of a baby's car seat in the back.

"Is everything okay, ma'am?"

"Daniel always said good things about you," she said, her hands clenched in front of her. "He said you took care of people."

Nick went still, although a thousand warning bells clanged inside his brain. "How did you know Daniel?"

"I need to talk to his wife," she continued, ignoring his question. "Brynn. Can you take me to Brynn? She'll be more comfortable if you're there. Daniel said you and Brynn were friends. He said you'd look out for her after…"

Her voice trailed off and her thin chest expanded with what looked like a painful breath. She had long brown hair and thin features, pretty in an unconventional way.

"After what?"

"He was going to leave her," she whispered, almost more to herself than him. "For me." Her eyes darted to the car's darkened interior again. "And the baby."

Brynn rubbed absently at her chest as she sat at the dining room table two hours later. Just when she thought her life couldn't turn any further in circles, there it went, spinning and tumbling like an avalanche. She expected to feel more.

She should feel something after receiving the news that her late husband hadn't only had one mistress at the end of his life, the woman who'd died in the accident with him. Apparently, if her late-night visitor was to be believed—and Brynn had no reason not to—Daniel had been planning to divorce Brynn and move on with another girlfriend, the one who had been nine-months pregnant with his baby at the time of his death.

She could feel the steady beat of her heart under her rib cage. Thump, thump, thump. Nothing else. From the moment Nick had called earlier, his voice low and apologetic as he explained the story of the woman who'd approached him in town, Brynn had gone numb. She'd put her son to bed with the same routine they had every night. Tyler had only recently started sleeping in his own bed again. The night his father died, he'd crawled under the covers with Brynn, and she'd allowed him to sleep there until he finally told her he was ready to return to his room.

"Would you like more tea?" she asked the woman sitting across from her.

"If you don't mind," Francesca answered, biting down on her lower lip. "The heat in my car hasn't been working, and it was a slow drive from Seattle. I can't seem to get warm."

Brynn could relate.

"I'll help," Nick offered, pushing back from the table at the same time Brynn straightened. She didn't need assistance pouring hot water from the teakettle but understood that wasn't why Nick wanted time with her in the kitchen alone.

"It's freaking me out how well you're handling this," he told her, as she turned on the gas stove's front burner.

"Would it make you feel better if I burst into tears or threw some plates against the wall?"

"Maybe." He ran a hand through his hair, which was already standing on end in messy tufts. "Hell, Brynn. I'm about to lose my mind over all of this. The woman who'd been with him in the car was bad enough."

"Katie," Brynn murmured, unable to help herself. "Her name was Katie."

She'd met the parents of the woman who had died along with her husband, about a week after Daniel's funeral, for coffee at Main Street Perk. They'd been a regular middle-aged couple, heartbroken over the loss of their only daughter. It had been a strange and surreal conversation. Katie, who lived in a town about thirty minutes from Starlight, had talked to her parents about her new boyfriend, but they hadn't met Daniel.

As far as the couple knew, Katie had been unaware the new man in her life was already married. They'd wanted Brynn to know that. To understand their daughter hadn't been a home-wrecker.

But even with the loss of Daniel so fresh and raw, blame hadn't been important to Brynn. Moving forward and helping Tyler move forward was her focus.

"We don't even know for sure the baby is Daniel's," Nick said, and Brynn could hear the desperation in his voice. The hope that her late husband had been someone different than the serial cheater they all knew him to be.

Brynn had given up hope years ago, and now was embarrassed she'd gone along with the farce instead of walking away.

The kettle whistled, and she poured the steaming water over a fresh tea bag that she'd placed in Francesca's mug, ignoring the way her fingers shook. The porcelain had a cheery band of snowmen circling it. Money had always been tight, and Brynn prided herself on the holiday decorations she'd purchased from thrift stores and garage sales, making their small house festive each season. Making things appear normal, even when they were anything but.

"The baby looks like a girl version of Tyler at four months," she said softly. "Don't pretend like you can't see the resemblance." She forced her gaze to Nick's. "She looks like her daddy."

He blew out an unsteady breath. "I hate this. I hate that he's done this to you. Obviously, Francesca is struggling, but I want to escort her to the town limits and tell her not to come back. I want it all to go away."

"You can't always get what you want," she answered, the decades-old song lyric somehow the story of her life.

"Tell me about it," Nick muttered, and the past curled between them like a plume of smoke, thick enough to choke her.

"She's alone." As Brynn picked up the mug, she concentrated on the warmth that seeped into her fingers. "Alone and scared. I'm not going to ignore her. That baby—Remi—is Tyler's sister."

"You're always a good person," he said, and his tone made the words sound like an accusation.

"I'm as human as everyone else," she told him. "You didn't turn her away, either."

"I wish I had."

"Stop. I know you don't mean it, Nick. You'll help her."

"I'll help you, Brynn. I'm here for you."

Those simple words, more than anything else, made emotion clog her throat, but she pushed it away. If she allowed the vulnerability locked up inside her any room to breathe, it might bloom and grow and crowd out everything else.

She moved toward the hallway that led to the dining room situated at the front of the house. "This mess is on Daniel, but I've got to clean it up."

"We," he corrected. "Even if I wasn't your friend, I have a duty as a public servant to help someone in need."

"Thank you," she said quietly but stopped at the dining room threshold, swallowing back a soft groan of empathy.

Francesca had moved to the wingback chair that sat in the corner of the room. In her arms, baby Remi was noisily slurping down a bottle of formula while her mother dozed. Francesca had propped a pillow underneath the arm that cradled the baby and the tiny girl didn't seem to notice that her exhausted mama had fallen asleep.

"Poor thing," Brynn murmured, remembering countless overnight feedings with Tyler. She'd breastfed, and Tyler hadn't taken a bottle until he was nearly a year old. It had been the two of them in the quiet nights and she'd woken any number of times with her baby in her arms after falling asleep for a few minutes.

"She looks exhausted," Nick said. "I don't think becoming a mother has been easy for her."

Francesca was a couple years younger than Brynn

according to what she'd told them. She worked as a waitress in a chain steak restaurant outside of Seattle. She'd met Daniel on one of his insurance sales trips into the city. He'd gotten a promotion a year and a half ago and those overnight forays to Seattle had become more frequent. Given his history, Brynn probably should have questioned him, but she'd enjoyed the evenings with Tyler when the tension of her marriage wasn't a palpable force in the room.

She placed the mug of tea on the table and approached Francesca and the baby. Remi looked content as she ate, her skin pink and a layer of downy hair covering her small head. She was nearly five months old, born only two weeks after her father's death.

Brynn's heart pinched at the baby's resemblance to her own son. She didn't relish the thought of explaining this situation to Tyler but hoped the idea of having a younger sister would ease the transition. Most people might think she was a fool, but this baby was a part of Daniel and that made her a part of Tyler. Brynn couldn't know whether helping her son to forge a relationship with his half sister would benefit him, but her heart told her it was the right thing to do.

If only Brynn had trusted her heart more often, she might not be in this situation in the first place.

"Hey," she whispered, touching a gentle hand to the woman's knee.

Francesca blinked several times before her gaze met Brynn's, panic and fatigue swirling like a cyclone. She glanced at the baby in her arms, almost as if she were surprised to find the child there.

"I'm sorry," she said. "It's been a day. I should go. I have a long drive back home."

"You can stay here tonight," Brynn offered without thinking about it.

She heard and ignored Nick's sharp intake of breath. "I'll get her a room at the Starlight Inn," he said in his official chief-of-police voice.

His commanding tone might work on some people—Francesca looked vaguely terrified—but it didn't faze Brynn.

"Don't be silly. We have a guest bedroom all made up."

"Are you sure?" Francesca asked, moving the bottle away from little Remi, who whimpered in protest.

Brynn thought about it for a moment, and for the first time since the accident, a sense of peace settled over her. Maybe it was the holiday spirit of generosity, but she knew taking in this lonely, frightened woman and her baby was the right thing to do.

"Yes," she answered.

"Thank you." Francesca's voice shook as she dashed a hand across her cheeks. "Also, I'm sorry

I had to be a part of Daniel hurting you. I'm sorry I believed the things he said."

"It's fine," Brynn assured the woman. "If you'd like, I can hold Remi for a few minutes while you get ready for bed? We could all use a decent night's sleep."

"Okay." Francesca didn't hesitate to hand over her daughter. "She probably needs her diaper changed."

Brynn sighed as the baby curled her hand into the front of Brynn's shirt. "I can handle that."

She purposely didn't look at Nick as she showed Francesca the guest bedroom and the hallway bathroom where she kept extra toiletries. Francesca hadn't brought an overnight bag but insisted she felt more comfortable sleeping in her clothes than borrowing pajamas from Brynn.

She gave the other woman a few minutes of privacy and returned to the dining room for the diaper bag.

Nick was waiting for her. "You can't do this," he said, arms crossed over his chest. "She's a stranger. You don't invite a stranger into your home."

"Thanks for your opinion," she answered, "and your work here is done. I'll call you tomorrow, okay?"

"Brynn, listen to me."

"Nick, look at the baby." She turned toward him fully. "She's Tyler's sister. Her mother is in a bad way, and I didn't get one weird vibe off her other than she was overwhelmed and tired as all get-out.

I remember those feelings. I still feel them most days. I'm not sending her away."

He stared at her so intensely that heat crept into her cheeks. "I'm running a background check on her before I head home, and I'll be back in the morning."

"Unnecessary," she muttered.

"Humor me, Brynn. Please."

Darn him and his manners. "I'll text you when we're awake."

He looked like he wanted to say more, but Remi sniffed and let out a cry. "She needs a diaper change."

"Call me if you need anything. I don't care what time it is."

Brynn nodded and let him out the front door, locking it behind him. After putting a fresh diaper on Remi, she lifted the baby into her arms again and snuggled the child closer. She didn't know what would come next but had no doubt this little girl was about to change everything.

Chapter Four

"Mommy."

Brynn blinked awake at the sound of Tyler's voice. Glancing at the clock on the nightstand, she held out her arms to her son. Just after six in the morning. Too early when it felt like it had taken hours for her to fall asleep last night.

"Did you have a bad dream, buddy?" She scooted over on the mattress to make room, but Tyler didn't climb in with her.

"I think Santa Claus came early," he told her, his voice solemn. He wore a stegosaurus T-shirt and striped pajamas that were too short for him now, although she'd bought them only a couple of months ago at the change of seasons. Often her days seemed interminably long, but time sped by when she marked it by her son's growth. His thick brown hair stuck up in sleep-mottled tufts, as it had almost every morning since he was a toddler.

Brynn commanded her fuzzy, sentimental brain to snap to it as she sat up in the bed. She couldn't imagine Francesca was already awake with how exhausted the woman had appeared last night, but if Remi had woken in the guest room downstairs, Tyler might have heard the baby crying.

This moment was what had kept Brynn awake. How would she tell her son that he had a half sister, let alone that the baby and her mother had ended up in Starlight? But the past five months had taught Brynn she was capable of handling more than she could have ever guessed.

"Did you hear something, Ty? I can explain—"

"Santa left us a baby," her son explained. "Under the tree."

A baby under the tree? Brynn was out of bed in an instant, panic blooming fast and hard in her chest.

"Someone spent the night here," she said, as she took Tyler's hand and tugged him forward. "A… um…friend of your daddy's. She has a baby, so it wasn't Santa. Did you see a grown-up, sweetie? I'm sorry. I thought I'd be awake to introduce you but—"

"Just the baby." Tyler followed her down the stairs, his fingers gripping hers tightly.

"Francesca?" Brynn called, as they got to the bottom of the steps. Silence greeted her. "Maybe she's in the bathroom or she went to her car for something."

"You're the only grown-up here."

Brynn shook her head. That simply wasn't possible.

But there was Remi, under the tree in her infant seat, small feet kicking as she contentedly sucked on two fingers. Brynn's panic morphed into a heavy sense of foreboding when she saw the folded slip of paper tucked into the padding next to the baby girl.

"Francesca?" she called again, even though at this point she didn't expect a response.

She let go of Tyler and dropped to her knees on the carpet in front of the tree. The baby's rosebud mouth curved into a smile when her sweet brown eyes fixed on Brynn. With trembling fingers, Brynn opened the paper and read the message written in a shaky scrawl.

Her lungs constricted as reality wrapped around her in a choke hold. Francesca was gone. According to the note, she'd left in the middle of the night, certain Remi would be better off without her since becoming a mother hadn't been part of Francesca's plan until the pregnancy happened.

"We should get her up," Tyler suggested, nudging Brynn's shoulder. "She's squirming like she wants out."

"That's a good idea, sweetie," Brynn said, trying not to sound as panicked as she felt. Was Francesca a danger to herself? What time had she left the house? How far had she gotten?

The baby gurgled happily as Brynn lifted her from the infant seat, kicking her legs and waving her arms. Brynn's heart felt like it was about to beat out of her rib cage.

"I wonder what her name is," Tyler said, smiling at the baby.

"Remi." Brynn ruffled her son's mop of hair. "Her name is Remi. The note said there are bottles for her on the counter. Let's see if she's hungry, and I'm going to call Nick and ask for his help with finding her mommy."

"Her mommy probably misses her already." Tyler led the way to the kitchen. "Did Daddy know Remi?"

"No," Brynn whispered, then cleared her throat. "She was born after your dad died."

There was so much about this situation she couldn't understand. How on earth would she explain it to a ten-year-old child? Instead of allowing herself to become overwhelmed, she did what she did best and focused on what she could control in the present moment.

Warming a bottle and feeding a hungry baby topped the list. Even as she heated water, Brynn was aware of the seconds ticking by. Every minute that elapsed was more time with Francesca out on her own, either getting farther away or potentially a danger to herself.

Brynn wasn't an expert on postpartum depression, but she certainly understood how it felt to be desperate and afraid of not being able to handle your own life.

When the water was the right temperature, she mixed the formula and moved toward a chair.

"Can I feed her, Mommy?" Tyler asked, still at her side.

"Sure, bud. Let's take her back to the family room because it will be easier for you to hold her on the couch. Babies seem small, but they get heavy in your arms."

"I'm strong." He scratched his belly as he walked next to her.

"Don't I know it," she murmured under her breath.

Brynn snatched her phone from the charger on the counter. Once she had Tyler settled with Remi, who still had yet to fuss, she showed him how to tip up the bottle to prevent pockets of air from forming.

She helped guide the nipple to the baby's mouth, and once Remi had begun to enthusiastically suck, Brynn sat back.

"She's hungry," Tyler said with a smile, as he glanced between Brynn and the baby. "Me, too. Will you make me a waffle?"

"Of course. Let me text Nick first." She figured

texting might be easier at this point because that way Tyler wouldn't hear the thread of alarm she doubted she could keep from her voice.

Forcing her features to remain calm for Tyler, she typed out a series of short messages to Nick that explained the situation and that she didn't want to talk about details in front of Tyler. Then she took a quick photo of Francesca's letter and forwarded it. Almost immediately, three little dots popped up on the screen alerting her Nick was responding.

Brynn could barely contain a relieved sob when the first message came through.

On my way.

She might want to keep her distance from Nick on a personal level, but Brynn knew he was a good police chief and trusted his judgment implicitly.

She placed her phone on the coffee table. Now that Nick was involved, she felt safe to focus her energy entirely on the baby.

"She's taken about half the bottle, so it's time to burp her." She reached for Remi, but Tyler handed her the bottle instead.

"Tell me what to do, Mommy."

Tears stung the corners of Brynn's eyes at how much Tyler seemed to like taking care of the little girl. "Put her over your shoulder while supporting her head and gently tap on her back." Brynn shifted closer, ready to help if the boy needed it.

He did as she said, and a few moments later Remi let out a massive belch that made both of them laugh.

When was the last time she'd heard her son's sweet laugh?

"She puked on me." Tyler made a face as he turned to look at his shoulder.

"Only a little spit up," Brynn assured him. "I'll grab a towel to clean you up."

By the time she returned, Tyler had the baby back on his lap. Remi stared up at him with wide eyes, like she'd never seen anything so fascinating. Then her face lit up with a gummy smile that Tyler returned with a broad grin of his own.

"She's pretty cute, even with the puking."

"You were adorable, too," Brynn told him, wiping the puddle from his shirt. "And you had horrible reflux that made you spit up all the time."

"Do all babies look alike?" His grip was sure as he held on to Remi. Brynn gave him the bottle and he tipped it up so the baby could finish it.

"Not all of them."

"This one looks like I did." He pointed to a framed photo that sat on the bookshelf next to the mantel. He'd been six months old when the picture was taken, only about a month older than Remi.

"She does," Brynn said softly, not sure when or

how to share the reason for the resemblance. This moment felt too soon, too fragile. There was too much unknown to drop a bombshell in the middle of it.

"She smells funny." Tyler wrinkled his nose.

"I'll change her diaper when she's done with the bottle." Brynn winked at him. "Unless you want to try that, as well."

"Nope."

"I don't blame you." She rose from the sofa. "I'm going to get your breakfast ready and then I'll take her from you. Okay?"

Tyler nodded, his attention focused on the child in his arms once again.

Brynn mentally calculated how long until Nick arrived as she toasted a waffle and started the coffeepot. She ran a hand through her hair, irritated that despite the chaos of the morning she still thought about how she must look. Tired, terrified and quite possibly like she'd been dragged to hell and back.

Too bad, she chided herself. She shouldn't—wouldn't—care what Nick thought of her appearance. Caring about Nick could only lead to more pain and she had more than her fill already.

Nick repeated the make and model of Francesca's car to the dispatcher and then disconnected the call as he parked in front of Brynn's house.

The sky was beginning to lighten, with shades of pink and purple stretching above him like slender fingers. He'd driven his truck instead of the department's Bronco this morning, but didn't doubt for a second the news of him paying an early-morning visit to Brynn Hale would be all over town by the time most people had finished breakfast.

At this point, he couldn't bring himself to care. He was too busy wishing he'd had a do-over on last night. One where he would have insisted on staying or making sure Francesca was stable. He would never have guessed the young mom would do something like this, but now he felt like he'd failed everyone involved, especially Brynn.

He hated that she had to deal with Daniel's baby with another woman on top of everything else she'd been through.

Climbing out of the truck, he noticed the curtains in the front window of the house across the street flutter. Karen Remington lived there, and the retired nurse was one of Starlight's biggest gossips.

Nick sighed. He hadn't planned to settle in his hometown, but he'd grown accustomed to it and his role in Starlight. In truth, he couldn't imagine living anywhere else. He loved the community and the sense of purpose it gave him to lead the town as police chief.

But sometimes a little anonymity wouldn't be the worst thing he could imagine.

Brynn opened the door as he approached, the baby cradled in her arms. The sight of her hit him like a swift punch to the gut, knocking the wind out of him. Brynn looked so damn beautiful standing in the doorway, her hair tucked behind her ears like she used to wear it back in high school. She wore a shapeless T-shirt and loose pajama pants, and somehow the casual intimacy of the outfit only added to the emotions assailing him.

"You look tired," he blurted out, then wanted to kick himself for once again saying the wrong thing to her.

"And panicked and overwhelmed," she added with an eye roll. "Excuse me for not making myself pretty for you, Chief. I was busy taking care of this little one."

"I didn't mean it like that." He shut the front door behind him as he followed her into the house. "You don't need to do anything to make yourself pretty, Brynn. You're already beautiful."

That was better, right?

Maybe not, based on the look she threw him over her shoulder. "Do you have any leads on Francesca?" she asked.

"Not yet. I've called the sheriff's department and state highway patrol. I haven't reached out to social services yet, but if she doesn't resurface soon, I'll need to alert them."

"What will happen to Remi?"

He watched as Brynn took a mug from the cabinet and poured coffee into it. How was she able to function so adeptly while holding the baby in her other arm and the chaos swirling around them? Was this some inherent gift mothers had?

"Thanks." He took the steaming mug she handed to him. "Foster care unless they can find a member of her family to take the baby. First they'll have to track down her records."

"I don't even know her last name." Brynn chewed on her lower lip. "There are so many things about last night I'd do differently if I had the chance."

"You can't change the past," he said after taking a long drink of coffee.

Her sky blue gaze darted to his, and the air grew charged between them.

"Trust me, I get it," she said quietly.

"Hi, Nick."

Nick turned as Tyler entered the kitchen and immediately walked to his mother's side.

"Hey, Ty. How are you doing with all this?"

"I fed her this morning and got her to burp." The boy tickled the baby's tiny foot. "She spit up on me, but it wasn't too gross."

Brynn smiled at her son in a way that made Nick's chest ache.

"That's impressive," he told the kid. "I'm not sure I'd want someone puking on me."

"Mommy said I used to spit up a ton. Way more than Remi. But I don't remember on account of I was little then."

"But you're a big help now." Brynn trailed a finger along her son's cheek.

"Did you find Remi's mommy?" Tyler turned toward Nick, his gaze serious.

"Not yet, but we're working on it."

"She can stay with us until her mom comes back." Tyler glanced up at his mom. "Right?"

"Of course, she's welcome here," Brynn answered without hesitation. "But she might have family or someone who's better suited to take care of her, sweetie."

"She likes me." Tyler's feathery brows furrowed. "And I like her. I didn't even know I liked babies but turns out I do. Colby Myers has a baby brother, but he cries all the time. Remi doesn't cry much."

"Not so far," Brynn agreed, sounding as unsettled as Nick felt.

The baby didn't look anywhere close to tears. She blew a few spit bubbles, then reached for Tyler.

"See, Mommy. She likes me."

"Because you're the best. Let's put her on the floor in the family room and you can play with her for a few more minutes before you head off to school. I think I have some of your old baby stuff in the basement that we can use for her while she's here."

"Cool," Tyler said and led the way from the kitchen around the corner to the family room.

Nick grabbed a fleece blanket from the back of the sofa and spread it on the floor. Brynn knelt down next to him and placed the baby on the soft fabric.

Remi seemed thrilled to have more room to stretch and wiggle. She kicked her legs and babbled when Tyler joined her on the blanket, making faces and grinning.

"She likes me a lot," the boy announced, clearly reveling in the baby's adoration.

"Who can blame her?" Nick asked, as he straightened.

Brynn crossed her arms over her chest as she watched the two children, a wistful smile playing at the corner of her mouth. A few years back Daniel had complained to a group of guys about Brynn wanting another baby. It had been at the bar after a softball game, and Nick had wanted to punch his supposed friend for the way Daniel insinuated that Brynn and Tyler were already too much of an inconvenience without adding another kid into the mix.

Brynn had always been a natural caregiver, sweet and nurturing when other kids—kids like Nick— were totally focused on themselves.

There was so much Brynn had compromised on when she'd married Daniel, and Nick still blamed himself for the turn of events that led to their quickie wedding.

He massaged a hand across the back of his neck, trying to rub away the irritation that pricked at his skin.

Brynn seemed to force her gaze away from Tyler

and Remi to give Nick a weak smile. "Could you help me bring up a couple bins from the basement?"

"Sure." He followed her out of the room and down into the cramped, unfinished space. "I'll call and check in with the station to see if she's gotten word from anyone after we get the stuff upstairs."

"I went through most of Daniel's things a month after the funeral. I don't remember any mention of a Francesca to help figure out her last name, but I can check his emails again." She sighed. "He was pretty good at covering his tracks, or maybe I was willfully ignorant to how unhappy he truly was with me."

Anger coursed through Nick, so hot and bright he was shocked it didn't light up the house's lower level. A few colorful rugs covered the floor and the cement block walls had been painted a cheery yellow. The washer and dryer were positioned on one wall with bins and storage shelves taking up most of the space on the other. Leave it to Brynn to make even a dreary basement look inviting. "Daniel's behavior wasn't your fault."

Her shoulders stiffened. "There's a baby upstairs whose presence in my house—in the world—would refute that statement. My late husband was adamant he didn't want other children. Apparently, the caveat was he didn't want children with me."

"You don't know the details of his relationship

with Francesca or what he thought about her pregnancy."

She exhaled a sharp laugh. "Thank heaven for small favors."

"I need to call child protective services, Brynn. Probably sooner than later for your emotional well-being."

She'd moved to the back corner of the basement, where gray plastic bins were stacked five high. "What does that mean?" she asked, standing on tiptoes to reach for the top container.

He moved behind her, once again wondering how a person who appeared so small and physically fragile could in reality be such an emotional powerhouse. His arms brushed her shoulders and the warm smell of vanilla drifted around him. Brynn's scent. How was it possible she still smelled the same as she had back in high school?

Okay, Nick wasn't an idiot. He understood how fragrance worked. His mom had been using the same brand of lotion since his childhood, and he'd always associate Olay with her. But this was somehow different, as if the scent were a part of her essence. Silly musing for a grown man.

Brynn shifted slightly, and Nick realized he'd gone still while he tried to untangle the reason her scent affected him on such a primal level. Although they didn't touch, his body cocooned hers in the quiet of the basement, the only sound their breathing and the hum of the furnace in the far corner.

"If you grab the top box," she said after a long moment, "I can get the one I need."

He lifted the container and moved away to set it down, filling his lungs with normal air. Damn if he didn't want to bury his face in the crook of her neck and stay there for as long as she'd let him.

"What did you mean about my well-being?" she asked again, as she handed him a heavy bin, twin spots of color flaming on her cheeks.

"We both know what that baby represents," he said, smacked back into reality once more. "You can't want her here."

At Brynn's shocked gasp, guilt assailed him. But he had to say the words. They both needed to deal with the truth of the situation.

"She's an innocent child without a mother at the moment." Brynn shook her head. "None of this is her responsibility. And she's Tyler's half sister. She's welcome here as long as needed."

"Are you going to tell him?"

She chewed on her bottom lip. "Yes. No. Once we have more clarity about what happens next."

They walked back to the stairs, and Nick stopped before climbing. He placed the bin on the bottom step and turned to face Brynn. She held another container, one labeled *unisex clothes*, as if she'd been anticipating what might come next. He took that tub from her and put it on the cement floor.

"What do you want to happen?" He used one finger to tip her chin toward him when she looked away. "Tell me, Brynn, and I swear I'll do everything in my power to make it come to pass. Anything."

There was a second of vulnerability that flashed in her gaze, like she might truly let him in to help. As if he might finally get a chance to make up for some of the mistakes he'd made in the past. He'd do anything for that chance.

Then she blinked and her gaze shuttered. She elbowed him out of the way and hefted the bin he'd left on the step into her arms. "I want what's best for Tyler and for the baby. It's all that matters."

Chapter Five

Three hours later, Brynn walked into her office at the Dennison Mill with an infant seat hooked on her arm. She'd been working full-time at the shopping area and community gathering place for only a couple of months but already felt a deep commitment to the project's success.

She'd grown up with Josh and Parker Johnson, the two brothers who'd bought and redeveloped the former lumber mill and turned it into a mixed-use space.

Brynn's unplanned pregnancy and subsequent wedding had derailed her plans to go to college like so many of her high school classmates. Daniel had gotten a job working for a local insurance agency while he went to school part-time. Brynn had stayed home with the baby, many hours on her own, and done her best to pick up odd jobs around town. Anything to feel like she was contributing.

She'd thought that would make Daniel happy. For the past decade, she'd worked her butt off to make her marriage a happy one, mostly for Tyler's sake. Still, she wouldn't deny she'd wanted more from her life and her relationship with her husband.

More than he could give apparently.

As much as she'd loved the kids and the staff at the school, it hadn't felt like enough. Certainly not enough to support herself and her son as a single mom.

She wanted something for herself.

Something more.

The job at the mill checked all the boxes, and she'd already planned a makers' market craft fair, a holiday wish list shopping event and a series of concerts by local performers. This holiday season was going to be the most successful she could make it. Josh, who was her primary boss now that construction was mainly complete, seemed to be satisfied with whatever she planned. Brynn wanted more than satisfied. She wanted to prove she could make the mill—and herself—successful.

A lot of her work could be done at home, but she liked to be on-site in order to talk to shop owners and customers. Little Remi stared up at her as she contentedly sucked on her pacifier. Did the baby realize her life had been turned upside down?

Of course not, but Brynn couldn't stop her eyes from pricking with tears every time she looked at the child. What was going to happen to her?

Nick had called a friend at the department of child welfare before leaving her house this morning. He'd convinced the social worker to drag her feet in processing the case, giving them at least the rest of the day to track down Francesca.

There had been no new leads on the missing mom, and Brynn wondered how hard to push to find her. As much as she hated to admit it, Brynn understood Francesca's need to flee. Being a new mother was overwhelming in the best circumstances, but to feel alone and scared could only magnify the anxiety. If Francesca hadn't wanted the baby in the first place, would she truly be able to give Remi the love and devotion she needed?

Brynn set the carrier beside the chair, then sat down at her desk and powered up her computer, forcing herself to put aside thoughts of the uncertain future. She was only going to stay at the office for a few hours, if Remi cooperated, and needed to get as much done as she could.

She logged on to her work email and her gaze immediately snagged on a message that was time-stamped an hour earlier. The subject line read *Remi*.

Heart hammering in her chest, she clicked on the

message. It was from Francesca, as she expected. The note explained Daniel's death had left a gaping hole in her heart and she couldn't imagine raising his baby on her own. She wrote that she needed time to gather her emotions, but in her current state of mind, she believed it would be better for Remi to be raised by people who could truly devote themselves to her.

Brynn forwarded the message to Nick's work email account and then pulled out her phone and texted him to let him know she'd sent it and that Francesca specifically asked for privacy to make a final decision in her own time.

Tyler's sister had been orphaned by her mother.

It wasn't a shock. Brynn had known deep in her heart Francesca wasn't going to come back and claim her baby. But she hadn't wanted to believe it, refused to consider what this meant going forward. Before she could truly process the ramifications of the inevitable truth of the situation, there was a knock on her office door.

She glanced up to find Mara Johnson waving from the doorway. Mara's hazel eyes widened, and her smile disappeared.

"What's wrong?" she asked, as she let herself into Brynn's office and closed the door behind her. "Has something else happened? Did they find Francesca?"

"I read an email she sent early this morning."

Brynn swiped at her cheeks even as she glanced at the little girl. "She's adamant about giving up the baby. I don't think it's postpartum depression. The email... She sounds resolute but sad and asks for time to contemplate the future. How can she feel resolved around something like this, Mara?"

"I don't know, hon." Mara came forward and gave Brynn a tight hug. "I can't imagine it, but know we're all here to help you and Tyler with whatever you need."

"Oh, lord," Brynn said with a laugh. "I must be a bigger mess than I thought if you're hugging me."

Mara stepped back. "I hug people. I'm warm and caring. A regular Mother Teresa." One corner of her mouth twitched because they both knew that, although Mara had a huge heart, her outer layer was as prickly as a porcupine. "Okay, the truth is you look like hell. Desperate times and all that."

"I appreciate the hug." Brynn gestured to the baby. "Look at her. She's so innocent and now so alone. I don't even know how to process any of this, and I've become quite the expert on handling untenable situations."

Remi was currently occupied with the toys that hung from the handle of her infant carrier. She swatted at a colorful butterfly, totally unaware of her circumstances.

It broke Brynn's heart.

"She's not alone. She has you." Mara handed

Brynn the brown bag she held. "I'm guessing you haven't eaten this morning. I brought blueberry muffins. You need food."

"Thanks." Brynn opened the bag and inhaled the delicious scent of Mara's freshly baked treats. The other woman might have a tough exterior, but she put heaps of love into every homemade goody she baked for Main Street Perk's two locations—both popular coffee shops owned by her aunt Nanci and Dennison Mill.

Mara had come to Starlight almost two years ago, emotionally scarred from her divorce but determined to make a new life for herself and her five-year-old daughter, Evie.

It probably seemed strange to some of the locals that Brynn's two best friends in town were Mara and Kaitlin Carmody, both women who were newer to Starlight. Being the girl who got pregnant in high school had changed more than Brynn's own life. It shifted how people in town saw her and treated her. Mara and Kaitlin didn't judge her for what had happened a decade earlier, and she need to create relationships with people based on the person she was now instead of who they wanted or expected her to be.

It was a little strange that her two friends had fallen in love with men Brynn had known since elementary school. Finn and Parker also happened to be Nick's two best friends, which made get-togethers with everyone sort of awkward. Good thing Brynn had become accustomed to awkward over the years.

For most of her adult life, Brynn handled things on her own. Daniel hadn't wanted to be bothered with mundane details and she'd had no desire to give her mom any more reason to judge her for the mistakes she'd made. Even after Daniel's death, she'd soldiered on, refusing to admit, even to herself, how his lies and callous treatment of her had worn away at her confidence until she was a shell of the woman she wanted to be. She'd become friends with Mara and Kaitlin over the summer, during an ill-fated stint as a coffee barista at Perk. The job hadn't been a fit, but she treasured her two friends and the unwavering support they gave her.

As she considered what to do next, Brynn broke off a piece of muffin. The sweet and tangy blueberries burst on her tongue, a tiny reminder that as numb as she felt, she was still capable of recognizing the good in life, even if it came in the simple form of a perfect muffin.

"Do you really believe Daniel was planning to leave you for Francesca and the baby?" Mara sniffed. "Your late husband was the worst kind of jerk, but I can't imagine even him leaving behind one family to commit to a new one."

"I don't know," Brynn answered honestly. "I turned a blind eye to rumors of Daniel's infidelity, and that's on me. But the story Francesca told, the way she seemed to love him, I'm not sure what to think at this point."

"You don't know her," Mara commented. "You don't know for certain she and Daniel were exclusive. I hate to say it, but without a DNA test, it's impossible to know whether Remi—"

"She's his." Brynn unbuckled the baby and lifted her out of the carrier. "She looks like him and almost exactly like Tyler did as a baby."

"That isn't a guarantee."

Brynn shrugged. "I'm not sure I can explain it to you, but there's not a shred of doubt in my mind this little girl is Tyler's sister."

"She's certainly a cutie." Mara's frown morphed into a smile as Remi gave her a wide grin. The pacifier dropped from her mouth, and Brynn reached out to catch it before it hit the floor. "I know this is a difficult situation, but it will work out. Once Francesca's parental rights are terminated, a wonderful family will come forward to adopt her. Or maybe there's someone in her family who—"

"I'm keeping her," Brynn whispered, then bit down on her lower lip. The thought had been ricocheting around her brain since she'd seen Tyler holding his sister. This baby was her son's family, and if her mother couldn't take care of her, Brynn would step in to be the mother she needed.

"You can't mean that." Mara blew out an unsteady breath. "Come on, Brynn. I know you have a huge heart, but it wouldn't be right."

Resolve made Brynn's shoulders stiffen. "Why not?"

"She's the baby of your late husband's mistress. A different woman than the one who was in the car when he died. How are you going to explain it?"

"I can't explain most of what I've experienced since the night of the accident."

Remi let out a small cry of distress, and Brynn loosened her hold on the baby. "Great. I'm starting out by squeezing her too tight. That will look amazing in my home study. Not." She patted Remi's back and cooed softly to her.

"Home study," Mara repeated, sounding dazed. "Have you thought about this?"

"I don't need to think. I know it's the right thing." She touched two fingers to her chest. "In here." The baby rested her head against Brynn's shoulder, and she took it as a sign. "I can do this. Tyler and Remi are siblings. It might be unorthodox, but I can give her a good life for as long as she needs me."

Mara shook her head. "I'm still not convinced, but you know I'll support you in whatever you need."

Glancing at her watch, Brynn let out a soft yelp. "Right now I need to get to the meeting about the wish list shopping event with the retail shop owners. I owe them an update on the marketing efforts."

"Let me watch Remi for you." Mara held out her hands. "I have some time before I need to get back downtown. I'll start calling people who might be able to help with baby supplies."

"I don't want to put you out," Brynn protested.

"Don't be ridiculous. I love babies."

Brynn chuckled.

"Okay, the only baby I've loved so far in my life is Evie, but I can handle this little one."

"Thank you." Brynn transferred Remi to Mara's arms. "Things are going great with the holiday campaign, so hopefully I won't be long. There are diapers and formula in the bag if she needs anything."

"Go," Mara urged, as she scrunched up her nose. "So you can get back soon."

Brynn took a deep breath as she grabbed a notebook and headed out of her office toward the banquet space at the end of the hall that also served as a meeting room. She glanced at her phone when it dinged to see a reminder pop up for the date she had tomorrow night. A date she'd no doubt cancel at this point.

If her dating profile had been pathetic before, this morning's turn of events pretty much sealed the deal on the coffin of her love life. Single working mom of a ten-year-old boy in a job she desperately wanted to be good at but felt underqualified for and overwhelmed by most days, plus an orphaned baby added to the mix.

Oh, yes. She was quite the catch. One most men in their right mind would throw back without a moment's hesitation thanks to all of the baggage that came with her.

"You can't be serious."

Nick's glare only intensified when Brynn shoved a microfiber rag and bottle of furniture polish into his hands.

"Be a friend and dust the bookshelves. The social worker will be here in a few minutes. I want her to see this place shine." Brynn glanced around the rarely used formal living room and grimaced. "Or at least I want it to smell shiny."

She'd always had plans to turn this cramped room into something besides the place where her mother's cast-off furniture went to die. The rest of the house reflected her tastes, but this room had been a forgotten item on her to-do list. At least now she had someplace to talk with the caseworker assigned to Remi that was out of earshot of Tyler.

The first thing her son had done when he arrived home from school that afternoon was place a gentle kiss on the baby's forehead. The gesture strengthened Brynn's resolve to become Remi's adoptive mother. She still hadn't told Tyler about his connection to the babe. She had no reason to believe she wouldn't qualify as a potential parent, but until it was more certain, she didn't want to say anything too revealing to her son.

"Your house is fine," Nick told her through clenched teeth. "It's your brain that's out of whack."

"Don't be rude."

"You can't adopt Daniel's mistress's baby." He shook his head. "Listen to how that sounds, Brynn."

She turned to him, hands on hips. "What do I care at this point?" After darting a glance toward the back of the house to make sure Tyler was still engrossed in his video game, she took a step closer to the police chief, who hadn't taken her announcement about her plans to make Remi part of their lives permanently half as well as Mara had.

"Do you know how many awful, pathetic stories around town of wasted potential and stupid choices involve me?" She lifted her hand to tick off her list. "The dumb girl who got knocked up her first time and forced unfortunate, noble Daniel Hale into marriage. Brynn, the pathetic young mom who spent every late night for years scrubbing toilets just to have enough money for her kid's birthday parties and new clothes at the beginning of each school year. Brynn Hale, the wife whose cheating husband was the worst-kept secret in all of Starlight." She leaned in, narrowing her eyes. "And there are heaps of badly kept secrets in this town."

"No one thought poorly of you," Nick insisted.

"Your right eyebrow is twitching."

He lifted a finger to his face. "What does that mean?"

"It's your tell, Nick. It always has been. When you lie, you get twitchy."

They were standing only inches apart, so close Brynn could see the flecks of gold in his brown eyes. His breath smelled like cinnamon gum, and it was like they were swapping childhood secrets all over again.

"I'm not lying." His strong jaw was set as if that could keep the rest of his face in line. "No one who means anything thought less of you because of Tyler."

"Then those same people won't find any fault with my decision about Remi."

"Point taken." His gaze stayed on hers as he reached out and touched the tip of one finger to the back of her hand. The touch was featherlight, but Brynn felt it like a missile had been launched within her body. He spoke the next words in hushed tones. "You've been through a lot this year."

"So has Tyler," she reminded him, trying to ignore his effect on her. "Do you know what having a sister would mean to him?"

"I'm thinking more about what it might do to you. I'm worried about you."

"That's not your job." She took a step away, but he grabbed her hand.

"We're friends. I care about you. I'm going to worry."

Her gaze dropped to their linked fingers. It felt strange—and somehow right—for Nick to be holding her hand. It felt good to be touched by a man, his calloused palm both rough and gentle against her skin.

She looked at him again, only to find his gaze trained on her mouth. The look in his eyes— longing if she had to guess—terrified and thrilled her.

Then the doorbell rang.

The social worker who stood on the other side, Jennifer Ryan, appeared to be in her midforties, a no-nonsense woman with a blunt bob and sharp features. She greeted Nick warmly and then he moved to the far side of the room to give Brynn some privacy with her.

Nerves fluttered through Brynn as she answered the woman's questions about Francesca and her late husband, as well as her current life as a single mom. The baby dozed in her arms, her grounding weight and the warmth of her small body a comfort to Brynn's frazzled nerves. When Brynn explained that she wanted to adopt Remi if Francesca didn't return in order for her to grow up with her half brother, the social worker blinked several times before answering.

"This is a unique situation, but I appreciate your willingness to step in. At this point, you're not approved as a foster parent." Jennifer flipped through the file she held on her lap. "We can begin the application paperwork, but it will take a couple of weeks for everything to be processed. Maybe longer at this time of year."

"But I can keep her in the meantime?" Brynn asked. A thread of panic snaked through her and she hugged Remi more closely. "You can talk to anyone in town about me or go through my closets. Whatever you need to do to put your mind at ease."

"I'm sure Nick would give you a reference, but it's not quite so simple." Jennifer's voice was gentle but firm. "The child must be placed with an approved foster parent. We'd like to keep her in this county, but the closest family available is in Pullman."

"No." Brynn swallowed back her emotions as she looked from the woman sitting across from her to Nick, who had moved to the edge of the sofa. "That's an hour away. We need Remi here with us. With me." Brynn couldn't explain her connection to the baby. She understood it made no sense, but much of her life hadn't since Daniel's death. All she knew was her heart told her keeping this child close was the right thing to do. For all of them.

Nick looked at her with a tortured expression, as if he could feel her pain. "There has to be another way," she said, as much to him as to the social worker.

"I'm sorry." The woman shook her head. "Unless there's an approved—"

"I'll take her." Nick massaged two fingers against his right temple. "I'm a licensed foster parent. Everything is up-to-date."

"Well, then." Jennifer gave a small smile. "Thank you, Chief Dunlap. I'll get the paperwork started and—"

"No." The word escaped Brynn's lips before she could stop it.

Both Nick and the social worker stared at her. "You have an objection to the police chief?"

Wasn't that question more loaded than a dirty diaper? Brynn shook her head. "Not to Nick but…" She turned to him. "You don't want to do this."

Although tension lines bracketed his mouth, he flashed a smile. "I told you I'd do anything to help you." He took the baby from her arms, balancing her far more naturally than Brynn would have guessed. "Remi and I will manage for a few weeks until you're approved." He leaned in. "No twitching at the moment, you'll notice. I want this, Brynn."

"Mrs. Hale?"

Brynn turned to the social worker, her mind dazed by a turn of events that she couldn't have expected even in the midst of so much emotional chaos.

"If there are no issues, I'm going to head out. I'll need you to come into the office for fingerprints.

A background check is standard, as well as an official home visit."

Issues. Yes. She had a million of them, but how could she give voice to a coherent thought when her mind refused to stop spinning?

"Fine," Brynn murmured.

"Thanks for stepping up, Nick." Jennifer stood and patted the baby's back. "I'll email the insurance information to you so you can schedule a routine checkup with a local pediatrician. You have my cell number if there are any problems."

"Appreciate it," Nick replied. "Say hi to your husband for me. I owe him a day of fishing come spring."

"He'll take you up on that."

Nick saw the social worker to the front door while Brynn stood rooted to the spot in the formal living room. She was afraid to move for fear she'd crumble to the ground.

As the door closed, Nick turned to face her again. "That went better than expected."

"Are you joking?" She felt her jaw drop and snapped it shut again.

"We can do this." He bounced the baby in his arms. "It will mean a lot of time together over the holidays, but that's not the worst thing in the world."

She continued to stare. Spending the next few weeks in close proximity to Nick might not be the worst thing, but it might take her down all the same.

Chapter Six

"She's precious, but are you sure you know what you're doing?"

Nick took a long pull off the beer he'd just opened.

"I have no idea what I'm doing, Mom. That's why I called you."

Alice Dunlap frowned, her thin brows pulling together as she glanced around the open-concept living area of his craftsman-style house. "The place will need to be babyproofed," she told him.

"She's five months old. I think the outlets are safe for now."

Alice sniffed. "Better to be safe than sorry."

The overarching mantra of his mother's life had

been choosing safe over sorry. But Nick had so many regrets from his choices, and not only the ones that concerned Brynn.

Top on the list was his brother's death eight years ago from a roadside bomb during his first tour in Afghanistan. Two years older, Jack had been serious and studious as a kid. Nothing like Nick who, much to the consternation of his physician father and town matron mother, hadn't taken anything seriously. Jack had gone off to Georgetown for college but dropped out after his junior year to enlist in the army. It hadn't made sense to anyone back in Starlight, but his brother had claimed that being in DC made him want to do his duty for the country.

Jack had been a true hero and look where that had gotten him. The opposite of safe and leaving everyone sorry in the wake of his death.

Nick had left college to return to Starlight six months later, when a heart attack stole his father's life. All desire to mess around had been obliterated in the wake of the pain he'd caused Brynn followed by the sorrow he felt after losing Jack. He knew he was at best a sloppy second for the role of good son, but he tried. All he could do was try.

"Right." Nick placed the beer on the counter. No sense finishing even one when he had no idea what the rest of the night would bring. "Thanks for rallying your knitting group to gather baby supplies." He gave his mom a genuine smile. "If those ladies were in charge of the world, it would be a much more efficiently run planet."

He'd called his mother from Brynn's house, without giving many details other than he would be fostering a baby girl and needed any type of clothing or furniture items she could round up. His relationship with his mom might not be the closest, but he knew he could depend on her and her network within the community.

"They were happy to help their favorite police chief," she said with a wave of her hand. "Although I'm going to hear about my lie of omission when the truth finally comes out about that baby."

"I appreciate that, as well." He moved toward the table and took the seat across from his mom. Teddy, snored softly on the dog bed situated under the window. "It's not exactly a secret, but I want to give Brynn the chance to tell Tyler the details before it hits the town phone tree."

His mother chuckled. "We text now or use the Starlight Facebook page."

"Even scarier," Nick muttered.

"Brynn is sure about adopting the baby?"

"As sure as I've ever seen her."

"That girl has always been stronger than people give her credit for. She's special."

"Are we talking people in general or someone in particular?"

Alice tapped a finger on the table. "The two of

you were so close growing up. I can remember all the time she spent at our house with you. She followed you around like you walked on water."

"Someone should have told me I couldn't. It would have saved me a lot of time trying not to drown."

His mother's eyes gentled. "You're doing okay."

Okay. Not exactly a ringing endorsement, but he'd take it.

"We both are."

"And Brynn," Alice added. "Especially given all she's been through. What does she think about you fostering the child?"

"She's not thrilled, but it's better than Remi being taken out of Starlight. I don't think she has a lot of faith in me."

Alice raised a brow.

"I'm not the same as I used to be, Mom. Hell, you said yourself, town residents respect the job I do. I'm working my butt off. Why can't people let go of judging me by my past?"

"Are we talking about people in general?"

He shook his head, amused and irritated at his earlier question being posed to him. "I want to help her."

"And you are. You will." Alice reached across the table and covered his hand with hers. She'd turned sixty last year, and while her hands were still delicate, with long graceful fingers and manicured nails, there were also subtle age spots and obvious veins covering the backs of them. Time didn't stop for anyone, even those rooted in the past.

"What are you going to do with Remi while you work?"

"I've called Mimi Briggs to see if she has room in her day care. A couple of the women from the department used her when their kids were little. I trust her." He glanced toward the baby monitor as it crackled on the counter.

"It's a shame to have another disruption for the child." Alice patted his hand. "Why don't I come over during the day and take care of her? At least for the first week."

Nick's heart slammed against his chest. He never would have expected his mom to make that kind of offer. "It's a big imposition."

"It will give me something to do—a good distraction. The holidays aren't my favorite time of year anymore."

Nick nodded. He struggled every year to make sure his mom didn't slip into a pre-Christmas depression. There were so many reminders of his dad and his brother and the traditions they'd had as a family.

A sharp cry sounded through the monitor, and he immediately stood. "I'd appreciate that, Mom." He leaned over and gave her an awkward hug. Nick still found himself unable to release the thought that she'd lost the wrong son. Nick's guilt and his mother's grief had coalesced to form an invisible barrier between the two of them. He loved her, of course, but recognized his love would never be enough to truly help her heal from the losses she'd suffered. "I need to go check on her."

She nodded. "I'll head home unless there's anything else?"

"You've done so much already. Thank you again."

"Nick, you're my son. I'd do anything for you."

Breathing through the rubber band that tightened around his chest, he nodded, then started for the stairs.

Remi was crying in earnest by the time he walked into the spare bedroom where he'd set up the crib his mom borrowed. The tiny wails cut through him, and he wondered at the wisdom of allowing his mom to leave.

What the hell did he know about taking care of a baby? He'd signed up for the foster program after his second year on the job, mostly so he could work with and mentor older kids and teens who might not have another positive role model in their lives. Despite his training, he'd never expected to be called on to serve in this way.

In theory, he knew what he was doing. In reality...

Alone in the quiet of his house, with only a dim night-light illuminating the room...he was as lost as if he'd been dropped into an unfamiliar forest in the dead of night.

He scooped her up and ignored the fact that his hands trembled. Of course, he'd seen friends and coworkers who were parents hold babies. He supported her head with one hand and her body with the other.

There was no funky smell like she had a dirty diaper or another sign of obvious distress. He'd fed her recently, a full bottle. But even as he cradled her close, her squalls became louder and more insistent.

"I wish I spoke baby," he murmured, racking his brain for any random baby-care tips he might have inadvertently picked up. As a single guy, Nick had never paid much attention to babies. He was going to be renting *Mr. Mom* and *Three Men and a Baby* as soon as he had a moment to spare.

Which might not be anytime soon if Remi didn't stop crying. He walked in a circle around the small space in front of the crib, jiggling her the way he'd seen his deputies do with their babies. "Please stop crying. Please stop crying." He said the words over and over and then put them to a melody. His own little desperate lullaby.

Oddly enough, as soon as he started singing, Remi's cries lessened. Nick was so shocked that he stopped, sending her into another fit of wailing.

Could singing be the secret sauce to settling her? He didn't know any kid songs or real lullabies so he launched into a version of his favorite Johnny Cash tune.

Remi continued to whimper for the first verse but by the time he got to the chorus about a burning ring of fire, she'd relaxed against him. Her breath came out in ragged sniffles as if she'd exhausted herself.

Did babies this young have nightmares? Or had she been roused by something—the sound of the old radiator or the house settling—and gotten spooked at being in a strange room.

He couldn't blame her, nor did he have any illusions he was some kind of talented baby whisperer. His voice was gravelly and off-key on certain notes, but the little girl in his arms didn't seem to care.

And all he cared about was the fact that she seemed to be falling back asleep. Not taking any chances, he sang about a fever hotter than a pepper sprout next. At the end, he glanced down and found her sleeping soundly, one small hand curled into the fabric of his flannel shirt.

As gently as possible, he lowered her into the crib once again. He stood watching for almost a minute, until he was certain she would stay asleep.

Then he turned to leave, only to stop in his tracks. His heart beat a wild rhythm against his rib cage as he realized that he and Remi weren't alone.

Brynn stood in the doorway of the bedroom, watching Nick like she was as spellbound by his singing as little Remi.

* * *

Brynn's breath caught in her throat as Nick walked toward her. Emotions assailed her from all directions, but even more powerful was the deep feeling of need that invaded every part of her body.

Without thinking, she reached for him, wrapping her arms around his neck and pulling him close. His hands splayed across her back, their strength and warmth an unexpected comfort. She rested her head on his shoulder and exhaled. The tension that filled her released its hold, and even if it was only for this moment, she appreciated any reprieve.

"Thank you," she whispered, although the words felt like a paltry choice to express how she felt.

She'd gotten to Nick's door as his mother was leaving. Although Alice Dunlap was one of the leaders in what passed for society circles in Starlight, she'd also been one of the few people in town who hadn't seemed to judge Brynn for her unplanned pregnancy. Brynn's mother had deemed Alice a snob and maintained that Nick's mom and her friends looked down their noses at women who weren't part of the town's "in crowd." Unlike her mother, Brynn had always admired Alice's grace and composure, even after enduring the back-to-back deaths of her older son and her husband.

"You're doing the right thing by that child," she'd said, as she gestured Brynn into Nick's house. "Don't let anyone tell you different."

"Nick is the one who saved the day," Brynn had responded and then jolted when she heard Remi's loud crying from upstairs.

Alice had given her a small smile. "He might need a bit of saving himself," she'd said before closing the front door.

Brynn had hurried up the stairs, more concerned for Nick than the baby. Babies cried and a tiny part of her envied Remi the freedom she possessed to let the world know her feelings. But Brynn didn't want Nick to regret his seemingly unplanned offer of help. This wasn't going to be an easy journey for anyone, and she would do everything she could to mitigate any difficulties.

If Nick had doubts about handling a baby, he was keeping them to himself. By the time she got to the small bedroom, he was singing quietly and Remi's cries had subsided. Brynn had stood transfixed by the scene in front of her.

The broad-shouldered, handsome-as-sin police chief crooning to the tiny babe in his arms. Was it possible for a heart—along with ovaries—to actually melt? If so, Brynn's would be in a sloppy puddle around her feet.

They stood together for several minutes, and Brynn drew comfort from Nick's big body and his heat. He felt both familiar and totally new. They'd spent so much time together as kids and teenagers, and she'd been half in love with him for most of her youth. She knew his scent and the way he took a longer inhale then exhale. But their bodies pressed together was a different sensation all together.

She tried to ignore her reaction, the way every inch of her skin tingled. It had been so long since she'd felt this way—if she'd ever felt this way.

On a shuttering sigh, she pulled back, afraid if she let herself stay with him for one more second, she might not have the strength to let go.

Nick didn't release her. Instead, he lifted one hand and smoothed his thumb across her cheek. "Your freckles have faded."

She opened her mouth to answer, but all that came out was a soft puff of air, so she gave a shaky nod.

"Brynn?"

Still no words, so another nod.

"I'm going to kiss you."

At those whispered words, she couldn't even manage a nod. Her body went on high alert. Involuntarily, she licked her lips, drawing a sexy half smile from Nick.

He leaned in, his breath fanning her mouth. "Was that a yes?"

She didn't respond, couldn't make a sound. Instead, she pressed her lips to his, a gentle touch that reverberated through her like a fanfare of fireworks.

A low groan sounded in the silence, and she realized it was Nick and not her. His palm cupped her

cheek in the way of kissing scenes from every ro-
mantic movie she'd ever watched. She should have
guessed that Nick Dunlap would kiss like a movie
star.

His mouth grew more insistent, and she gladly
opened, inviting him in deeper, caught up in the taste
of him and the way the kiss made her come alive.

She'd felt numb for the longest time.

How was it possible to be in her twenties and feel
like her lady parts had already shriveled up? Now
everything inside her seemed to bloom like desert
flowers after a heavy rain.

She wanted this. This moment. This man. So
much more.

The thought of more in her already complicated
life made warning bells go off in her fuzzy brain.
Then Remi let out a small cry in her sleep, which
had Brynn yanking away. Nick wasn't for her. She'd
learned that lesson years ago and couldn't afford to
repeat her past mistakes.

Especially not when the baby sleeping a few feet
away needed her. Needed both of them.

He released her without hesitation, color high on
his cheeks and his chest rising and falling like he
couldn't quite catch his breath.

At least Brynn wasn't the only one affected.

She gave a wan smile and turned for the stairs,
hoping he believed her fast retreat was so they didn't
wake the baby by speaking.

In truth, she needed time, even a few seconds, to gather her wits. What the heck had she been thinking kissing Nick?

Where could that lead? No place good for her heart or her peace of mind.

When she got to the kitchen, she stopped, then pivoted toward him.

"That can't happen again," she said at the same time he blurted out, "I've wanted that for so long."

Brynn swallowed when it felt like her heart leaped into her chest. "Excuse me?"

"Never mind." Nick dipped his chin and gave a small shake of his head. "You're right. It was a mistake. Forget about it."

He'd wanted to kiss her? That didn't make sense. Nick had barely spoken more than few a pleasantries to her since high school. Of course, their paths crossed in a town the size of Starlight. He'd been one of Daniel's friends. Brynn's friend. But despite the crush on him that had felt so overpowering when she was younger, he'd never looked at her in that way. Or so she'd thought.

She didn't want to forget even if she didn't believe it could go anywhere. Her body hummed with awareness, but she ignored it. If nothing else, Brynn was a master of ignoring what didn't serve her. "Our focus needs to be on Remi," she said, careful to keep the emotion out of her voice.

"Yep," he agreed, his lips barely moving.

"I came over to check on her," she continued. "On both of you. Not for..." She waved her arm between the two of them and then quickly realized it looked like some sort of spastic bird, wing flapping, and pulled it down to her side.

"Understood."

"Your mom let me in."

"I figured."

"And I heard Remi crying so I came upstairs." She forced her lips together. Nick wasn't an idiot so he didn't need her stilted play-by-play.

"I hated hearing her cry that way."

"You comforted her," she reminded him, then exhaled a laugh. "I forgot how much you love Johnny Cash."

"The man in black never fails." One side of Nick's mouth quirked. "Unlike some of us."

"I'm glad your mom was able to help round up supplies."

"She's going to watch the baby while I'm at work." He ran a hand through his hair. "At least until I can arrange other childcare."

"I'll help, too. Of course." She nodded, more to herself than him. "I can't tell you how much I appreciate you fostering her until I can be approved."

"It's not a big deal."

"It's huge." She stepped forward, reached out an arm, then drew it back into her body. Touching him would get her nowhere.

"Have you told Tyler?" he asked quietly.

She shook her head. "I meant to tonight, but every time I opened my mouth, I started to cry. It's ridiculous. I've cried more in the past twenty-four hours than I did after Daniel died."

"It's been a lot to process."

"We both know how things work in Starlight. I have to talk to my son before word gets out about Remi."

"That's part of why my mom is going to stay with her during my shifts," he replied. "She won't say a word to anyone."

"Your mom looks good. Are things okay between the two of you?"

The question felt inadequate given all she knew about Nick's family history. His older brother had been the golden child, leaving Nick in the role of family clown. Brynn had always known there was more to him, deeper wells of emotion and ambition, but he refused to shake his devil-may-care personality. Then Jack was killed and Nick's father had a massive heart attack six months later. Alice sank into a deep depression that was spoken of in hushed tones in grocery store aisles and after Sunday service.

Nick returned to Starlight and became a deputy, quickly earning a promotion when the longtime police chief retired. At the time, Brynn had been busy with a toddler and trying to make something of the cards life had dealt her.

Their paths had gone in different directions, and she'd forced herself to disregard how important he'd been in her life. Her best friend.

At the moment, memories assailed her from every side, especially when he shrugged and offered her the self-deprecating smile he'd perfected at a young age.

"I think so. I'll never be Jack, but no matter how much we both want him to still be here, I think she's come to terms with that. I have."

"You're a good man, Nick. You always have been."

His gaze grew more intense as he studied her. "Not always."

Heat flushed along Brynn's skin. She'd spent a decade believing she was over her feelings for this man, only to discover how quickly they could blossom again.

"Close enough," she muttered, then took a step away. Needing to get out of the house before she did something stupid like launch herself at him. "Mara is at my house, so I should go. Like I said, I wanted to stop by and make sure you didn't need help. Clearly, you're doing fine without me."

"I wouldn't exactly say that." Nick's voice was a low rumble.

"Then neither of us should say anything more."

His expression went blank, as if he understood her meaning but didn't like it. But he followed her to the front door without speaking.

"I'll check in tomorrow," she said at the edge of the porch. "I'd like to spend time with Remi while my foster application is in process so it's not such a big transition for her. If that's okay?"

"That would be good," he said.

"Good night, then." She lifted a hand and he waved in response.

Hurrying down the walk toward her car, Brynn was grateful for the cool night air surrounding her. She needed all the help she could get so she didn't overheat from the desire that stretched like an electric charge between them.

Chapter Seven

"Why can't we keep her now?"

Brynn placed a plate with grapes and a peanut-butter sandwich in front of Tyler, then took the seat across from him at the kitchen table.

"Because the state has a process for approving foster families. She's going to stay with Nick until my application goes through. Are you sure you're okay with this, bud? I know it's a big shock. If you have questions…"

"Would Remi still come to live with us if Dad was alive?"

The possibilities of what the future might have held if Daniel hadn't died ricocheted through Brynn like a bullet, tearing flesh and wreaking havoc on her insides. She kept her features neutral as she met her son's open gaze.

There was no anger or bitterness in his dark eyes. Only curiosity, as if they were riddling out a puzzle together.

"I'm not sure what would have happened, but she's your half sister. That wouldn't have changed."

"Mike DeMarco has a little sister. She's three and always messes with his Legos. She destroyed the Millenium Falcon he built, and it took him like a gazillion hours to finish it."

"We've got some time before Remi could get into your toys, and we'll make sure to put up anything that's special to you, so she knows not to play with it."

Tyler's mouth dropped open and he sat up straighter. "Oh, no, Mommy. We have a big problem."

Brynn braced herself. She suspected Tyler's easy acceptance of the news that Remi was his sister might have been initial shock and not his true reaction to a massive shift in both of their lives.

"Tell me." She nodded. "You can talk to me about any problem."

"Will Santa Claus know to find her here?"

Brynn blinked, then blew out a surprised huff of laughter. "Yes," she assured him. "Santa Claus will know."

Tyler took a big bite of his sandwich and asked around a mouthful of food, "How?"

"Um…" Brynn's gaze caught on Santa's jolly face grinning at her from the dish towel that hung over the handle of the oven. She decorated for the holidays in every room and had probably gone overboard this year, wanting their house to be festive and happy no matter how she felt on the inside.

"The elves will update him," she said finally. "They keep track of all the children around the world."

"Do you think Remi has sent him a letter?"

Brynn shook her head. "I don't think babies send letters to Santa."

"Then how will he know what to bring her on Christmas? Like he's going to know that I want Legos and a remote control race car and a microscope."

"Hold on." Brynn held up a hand. "I don't remember seeing a microscope on your list for Santa." They had a tradition of writing the letter on the day after Thanksgiving. This year it felt like Tyler had taken an especially long time to come up with his list and asked her several times if she thought the items on it might be too expensive.

His concern just about broke Brynn's heart. She'd assured him that the gifts on his list were well within Santa's capabilities and the look of relief on his face was both comical and disturbing. She knew it was only a matter of time before he stopped believing in that particular part of the magic of Christmas. And while it would be a relief not to go through the trouble of hiding gifts and secretly shopping, she wasn't quite ready to check that childhood milestone off the list.

"I added it at the last second before we sealed the envelope and mailed it." He looked embarrassed and a little concerned. "Max stood up in math a couple of weeks ago and yelled out that there's no such thing as Santa. He made Juliana Dalton cry."

"That wasn't very nice." Brynn felt her eyes narrow. She'd like to have a word with Max. "What did you think when he said that?"

"I thought he was a big fat liar," Tyler confided, tearing the crust off the end of his sandwich before taking a final bite. "I told him so, too."

"No name-calling," Brynn reminded him.

"Yeah, I know." Tyler gulped down half his glass of milk, then wiped his sleeve across his upper lip. Good thing Brynn had placed the napkin next to his snack plate. "I thought if I sneaked something on my list that you didn't know about, I could prove Santa was real."

"Well...yes, that would work." Brynn racked her brain for where she'd hidden Tyler's letter when he gave it to her to mail. Normally, she read over it several times during the weeks leading up to Christmas to make sure she didn't miss anything. This year, she was operating on autopilot in most areas of her life, trying to balance her new job with single motherhood and not reveal any of the massive cracks in her armor to the outside world. How many other little things had she missed or overlooked in her need to keep up the facade of normal?

The possibilities were endless.

"Remember, bud, Santa lives in your heart. It's the spirit of Christmas that allows people to believe in him." She stood from the table and moved to give her son's small shoulders a squeeze. "I don't know why Max doesn't believe, but Christmas isn't about proving the truth beyond a shadow of doubt. It's about faith."

She smoothed the hair out of Tyler's eyes as she gazed down at him. "Does that make sense to you?"

"I guess." He pushed back his chair and grabbed his plate off the table. "Can we still write a letter for Remi?"

"Sure."

"Can we go visit her now?"

"Visit?" Brynn swallowed. Nick would be at work and his mom at the house, so maybe this was the right time to go over. In all honesty, she hadn't expected her son to take all of the impending changes to their lives in stride.

"If you bring your laptop, I can show her some toys for babies. Maybe she'll kick her feet or something to tell me what she wants on her list."

"Maybe," Brynn agreed. "You do homework, and I'll call Nick's mom and ask if it's okay that we stop by."

Tyler placed his plate and glass in the sink. "Does Grandma know about Remi?"

"No one does yet." Brynn kept her tone light even when panic flooded her. "But I'm sure people will find out soon, and I'll call your grandma tonight. I wanted you to be the first to know."

Tyler nodded and Brynn appreciated his easy manner, even though she knew he didn't understand the full impact one small baby would have on their lives. Brynn did her best to put aside some money toward Tyler's college fund every month. Now, in addition to providing for Remi, she figured she should start a new fund for both of the children to use for therapy later in life. She couldn't believe things could be this easy. Nothing in her life up until this moment had been.

"I always wanted a little brother or sister," Tyler told her.

A lump formed in her throat. "I didn't know that, bud."

"I have one now, and I'm going to teach her all the things about being a kid." He drew in a deep breath, swallowed, then opened his mouth and let out a loud series of belches. "Like how to burp the ABCs. I got up to *G* the other day at recess."

"Nice work," Brynn told him with a grin. Her mother would tell her to try to curb that kind of behavior, but Brynn figured Tyler had enough of his childhood stolen from him with his father's death.

Why sanction a bit of silly fun? "But stop delaying on the homework."

He groaned. "We're doing times tables in math. I hate multiplication."

She lifted a brow. "It doesn't get done if you don't do it."

"Fine," he grumbled. "I'm going, but you can't make me not hate it."

"I'd never try," she promised. When he'd disappeared up the stairs, she grabbed her phone and sent off a quick text to her mother, asking for Alice Dunlap's cell number.

Within seconds, her mother replied, sending the number with the question WHY? in all caps. Whitney Roberts did a lot of screaming via text. Unlike Brynn, her mother had a big blustery personality and had no problem expressing her emotions. Too bad most of them were judgmental and negative when it came to Brynn.

She responded she had a quick question about the local church choir's Christmas concert. That seemed like an easy enough answer. Alice had been in charge of the concert for ages, and this year the event was being held at the Dennison Mill.

She waited for her mother to reply, to ask about Brynn's job or how she could help with the event. Or to ask about her only grandson or...

The screen remained empty and Brynn cursed the disappointment that crested inside her. She should be used to her mother's disinterest in her life. That didn't make the indifference hurt any less, even after so many years.

With a sigh, she touched her thumb to the hyperlink of Alice's number and lifted the phone to her ear.

The smell of garlic and tomato sauce enveloped Nick the second he opened the door from the garage into his small laundry room. His stomach grumbled in response, a sharp reminder of the chaotic day he'd had and the fact that there hadn't been a minute to stop for a bite to eat since he arrived at the station that morning.

Teddy padded into the room, tail wagging, and nudged Nick's leg, then went to sit by his dog bowl. Nick wasn't the only hungry guy in the house.

In addition to responding to a car crash out on the main highway and a possible burglary at a farm outside town, he'd had meetings with the chamber of commerce and the mayor's communications director. In fact, Nick might still be at work if one of his deputies hadn't agreed to come in early.

Nick hated asking for help, but he also didn't want to burn out his mom on her first day watching Remi. The baby had been asleep when Nick left for work, and the truth was he wanted to see her. Yes, he trusted his mother, but the baby was his responsibility and he was well past the age of shirking his duties.

He walked into the kitchen, but instead of his mother, Brynn stood at the stove, stirring something in a large pot that he assumed was the source of the amazing scent permeating his home.

She wore a Starlight High School sweatshirt and jeans that hugged her curves. Her hair was loose and her feet bare. She looked casual and comfortable and the scene in front of him was the sexiest thing Nick had ever seen.

Damn, he must be getting old if domestication was a turn-on. Although in his heart, he knew the reaction had more to do with Brynn being at the center of it than anything else.

A few feet away, Remi sat in the high chair his mother had procured, contentedly gnawing on some kind of toy.

"Hi, Nick," Tyler called, waving to him from where he was coloring at the table. "Mom's making spaghetti."

Brynn spun toward him, yanking the wooden spoon to her chest like a shield.

Nick cringed as red sauce splattered down the front of her sweatshirt. "Sorry." He held up his hands, palms out. "Didn't mean to startle you."

"I didn't hear you come in." She pointed to Teddy, who'd followed Nick into the main house. "He seems to be a barker when people come to the door."

"He knows the sound of my car." Nick bent and scratched between the dog's ears. "Is my mom here?"

"Not anymore." A blush staining her cheeks, Brynn placed the spoon on a plate next to the stove and grabbed a paper towel, blotting at her sweatshirt. "Tyler and I stopped by to see Remi and while we were here, your mom got a call from Jolie Patterson. Dave fell off a ladder while putting up Christmas lights and Jolie was afraid he broke his hip. Your mom asked if I could stay so she could meet them at the hospital and sit with her."

Nick frowned. "I drove by the Pattersons' a few days ago. They've already got so many lights on the house you could practically see it from space."

"You know how Jolie likes to decorate and Dave likes to make Jolie happy. I'm sorry I didn't think to warn you we'd be here."

"Making dinner," he added, as he moved toward her. He took a clean dishrag from a drawer, wet it under the faucet and handed it to Brynn. "This might work better than paper towels."

"Thanks." She concentrated on the stains on her sweatshirt instead of meeting his gaze. "I'm sorry if making myself at home is a problem. Tyler and I always eat at six, so I thought…"

"It's fine." Nick reached out a hand and tipped up her chin. "My house hasn't smelled this good… well…ever. I love spaghetti."

She chuckled, and the sound reverberated through

him like music. "That was obvious since jarred sauce and frozen meatballs seemed to be the only thing other than condiments in your pantry and fridge."

"Is it almost time to eat?" Tyler asked from the table.

"Yes." Brynn turned to the boy. "Wash your hands and you can help set the table."

"What's sweet Remi doing?" Nick looked more closely at the baby. She was chomping on the plastic toy she held with surprising gusto.

"It's a silicone teething ring that I put in the freezer for a few minutes so it would be cold on her gums."

"Mom said I could help feed her dinner," Tyler announced, as he walked by on his way to the sink. "Since she's my sister and all."

Nick felt the boy's gaze on him, primed for a reaction.

"She's a lucky kid to have you for a big brother, Ty."

That earned a cheeky grin. "Yeah, I know."

"I'm going to change clothes and wash up, too." Nick moved to the high chair and bent to place a soft kiss on the top of Remi's head. She smiled and held out her toy to him. "You keep that, sweetheart. Looks like you're having a grand time with it."

"Any chance I could borrow a shirt?" Brynn asked. "I'm kind of a mess with sauce all down the front of me." Her tone was casual, but Nick could hear something in it. A thread of sensuality that had awareness alighting through him.

"Sure. I'll grab something upstairs for you." He avoided looking directly at her. Despite the shapeless sweatshirt, he had no problem envisioning the curves it covered. Imagining those curves covered by something he wore made his blood run hot. Could he be more pathetic? "Be down in a few."

In his bedroom, he changed out of his uniform and into a T-shirt and jeans. He washed his hands in the bathroom sink and splashed water on his face. A cold shower wouldn't be out of the question at the moment. *Get a hold of yourself,* he chided. There was nothing about this situation that would appear the least bit seductive to an outside observer.

And everyone knew Nick was a committed bachelor. Hell, even the town cronies, who loved to matchmake as much as they loved a rousing night of bunco, had given up on him. One pseudo-family dinner with people who didn't even belong to him would change nothing.

Flannel shirt in hand, he reentered the kitchen, and his breath caught in his throat. All coherent thought dissolved at the sight of Brynn in a thin white tank top, placing plates on the table while Tyler trailed behind her with forks and knives.

Was this how Ward Cleaver felt every time he walked into the house and found June engaged in some mindless domestic task? No wonder the man had seemed so happy during all those late-night kid channel reruns Nick watched with his brother when they were kids.

As if sensing the weight of his stare, Brynn turned and offered a tentative smile. "I hope you're hungry," she said, then bit down on her lower lip. "We really have invaded your space."

"I appreciate the meal." His voice sounded too gravelly, even to his own ears, and he cleared his throat. "Here's a shirt."

Her fingers brushed his as she took it, and he wished he knew if the blush that stained her cheeks was from her reaction to him or strictly a result of working in the kitchen.

"What's your wee sister having for dinner?" he asked Tyler, needing to get his mind off Brynn's body.

"Green beans and rice cereal," the boy answered with a grimace. "So yucky."

"Not to a baby." Brynn put a hand on her son's shoulder. "Concentrate on your food first and then you can feed Remi."

"What can I do?" Nick's stomach rumbled as he took in the inviting spread of food on his normally barren table. A big bowl of noodles, meatballs and sauce sat in the center with a salad and a basket of garlic bread flanking it on either side.

"Do you have salad tongs?" Brynn asked.

"How about two forks?"

She grinned. "Perfect."

He grabbed the utensils and raised a brow in Tyler's direction. "One scoop of salad or two?"

The boy climbed up onto his chair across the table. "None."

"One," Brynn corrected.

Tyler rolled his eyes. "A tiny scoop."

Nick dished out salad to each of them while Brynn filled bowls with the pasta and passed around the bread basket.

"I can't believe you came up with a dinner this good from stuff I had in the house. I didn't realize I'd bought lettuce."

"Your mom told me it was in the fridge. She brought veggies over this morning because she guessed you wouldn't have any."

"Because vegetables are nasty," Tyler offered.

"Amen, little dude." Nick grunted when Brynn's toe connected with his shin. "I mean, not all of them. And they're good for you, so we all need to eat at least one scoop."

He looked at her across the table for confirmation he'd redeemed himself.

Brynn shook her head, but her lips twitched and somehow that felt like a win. He wanted her to smile more, and he wanted to be the man who made her smile.

"Where'd these place mats come from?" He ran a finger along the edge of the woven fabric.

"I found them in one of the drawers."

"Huh." He owned place mats. Who knew?

Remi let out a cry of delight when Brynn dipped a spoon into the small cereal bowl and offered her a bite.

They'd gone over her feeding schedule and the variety of foods she could have at five months with the social worker, but Nick was still relieved to have an actual mother here to oversee the baby's first dinner in his house.

"You like it," Brynn told the girl. "Remi is such a good baby. You're going to grow big and strong like your brother."

"She's even messier than me," Tyler said with a laugh, then shoved half a piece of garlic bread into his mouth.

"Slow down," Brynn admonished gently.

"I want to finish so I can feed her."

"You'll have plenty of opportunities to feed her." Brynn wiggled her eyebrows. "Don't forget diaper duty."

Tyler made a face. "Gross."

"I can confirm gross," Nick told him with a wink. "Last night she had a blowout."

"A blowout," the boy repeated, sounding mesmerized.

"Poop halfway up her back."

"Seriously? Mom, did I ever have a blowout?"

"You were legendary," Brynn answered, laughing. "And your timing was impeccable. Something about the car seat got you moving like nothing else. I can't tell you how many times we'd pull out of the driveway only to pull right back in."

"She gets her blowout talent from me."

Brynn wrinkled her nose. "I'm not sure that's a talent."

"She still takes after me." Tyler shoved a final meatball into his mouth, wiped his hands on a napkin, then pushed back from the table. "Can I have a turn feeding her? I even ate the salad scoop." He darted a wicked side glare toward Nick. "Which wasn't small at all."

"Nice work with the salad," Nick said and Tyler nodded, seemingly mollified by the praise.

Nick ate his dinner and watched as Brynn instructed her son on feeding the baby. As soon as Tyler moved into Remi's line of sight, she squealed with delight and pumped her whole body back and forth, as if a current of electricity coursed through her. It was hard to believe the two of them could have formed a bond in such a short time, but the connection was undeniable.

In the space of one day, Nick's life had been turned upside down. Wednesdays normally meant dart night at Trophy Room. He'd begged off tonight without explaining his reason. Remi's presence would be public knowledge soon enough, but he wasn't up for fielding questions he didn't have the answers to. No one would believe he'd willingly become the foster parent to an orphaned baby.

But no one understood what Brynn meant to him.

He'd denied the feelings for so many years that even he couldn't quite comprehend how quickly she'd once again become essential to him.

It was different than it used to be, and not just because of the divergent paths their lives had taken. He'd been a young, stupid, selfish kid back in high school, his ego preventing him from believing that his life would ever be anything but perfect.

Brynn had been a steady presence in his life, and he'd been an idiot to believe that would never change.

His heart clenched as Tyler dissolved into a fit of giggles when Remi took a bite, then let it dribble out of her mouth.

The baby grinned and smacked her hands against the top of the high chair table.

"I think she's had enough," Brynn said, humor lacing her tone, when Remi repeated the action two more times.

"She's funny," Tyler observed. "Was I a funny baby?"

Brynn gave his cheek a quick kiss. "You could make me laugh harder than anything."

The boy shrugged away from his mom's embrace even though it was clear he enjoyed the attention. "Did I make Dad laugh, too?"

The band around Nick's chest tightened for an entirely different reason as Brynn's smile turned wistful.

"All the time," she answered. "Your dad thought you were the funniest, smartest, cutest baby in the whole world."

"I wish he was here to meet Remi."

"Me, too, sweetie," Brynn whispered, reminding Nick that as perfect as this night felt, this wasn't his family. They didn't belong to him.

In a few weeks, when Brynn's application was approved, Remi would be gone from his home and Brynn would continue building a life with her two children. And Nick would be alone again.

Chapter Eight

Nick looked up from his computer two days later as the door to his office opened. "I'll be done in a..."

He swallowed back a groan as Finn and Parker shot him twin death glares. Finn closed the door, giving Nick the briefest glimpse of the curious stares from his assistant and the deputies in the station's outer office.

"It's not a big deal," he said, pushing the chair away from the desk. No point bothering to pretend he didn't understand why his two friends had cornered him at the station. "I was going to tell you when the time was right."

"There is no right time for you to be fostering

Daniel Hale's illegitimate baby." Parker crossed his arms over his chest, the tie knotted at his neck shifting in the process. Parker's big-city style had relaxed since he'd returned to Starlight, but he still favored tailored suits during the workweek.

"It's not her fault her dad was a two-timing loser." Nick shook his head. "I'm doing this as much for Brynn as for the baby."

"You don't have any experience with babies," Finn reminded him.

"Neither do you," Nick shot back.

Finn handed Nick and then Parker a wrapped sandwich from the brown bag he carried. "Which is why I didn't agree to foster one. Eat the chicken salad and come to your senses, man."

"If you're aware I've got her, then I'm sure you've also heard that Brynn is planning to adopt her if the mother doesn't return."

"Also irrational," Finn said.

"Don't call Brynn irrational," Nick warned. "She's the most levelheaded person any of us know."

"She wants to raise her cheating husband's—"

"Stop." Nick stood. "We all understand the situation. Brynn is doing what she thinks is right for Remi and for Tyler. It's not anyone's place to judge. We need to support her, to support all three of them."

"Did you give that line to Mara?" Parker asked,

shaking his head. "She said almost the exact same thing to me this morning."

"Kaitlin, too." Finn scrubbed a hand over his jaw. "I admire Brynn's devotion to mothering an orphaned child, but I don't like that you're involved."

"Why not?" Nick demanded. "I'm the police chief. My job is to take care of the community."

"Which has nothing to do with it." Parker pointed a finger at him. "She's a baby, Nick. A human being. Someone you have committed to keeping alive for the indefinite future in order to impress a woman."

Irritation made his skin flush hot. "That's offensive to both me and Brynn."

"Not our intention," Finn insisted. "At least where Brynn is concerned. But you, my friend, are not equipped to be responsible for a baby. You know nothing about babies."

"As a matter of fact…" Nick jabbed his finger into the air. "I watched *Three Men and a Baby* last night. Even I know you don't dry a kid's bottom by lifting them over a blower in a public bathroom. Those things spew a crap ton of bacteria into the air."

Parker swatted Finn's arm. "We may have underestimated the severity of the situation. He's talking about germs in public restrooms."

"What the hell is the problem?" Nick demanded.

"Just tell Brynn you're in love with her," Finn shouted.

Nick cursed and stalked around the side of his desk. "Keep it down. The last thing I need is that hitting the gossip train in town, especially when it's not true."

"Come on," Parker urged, running a hand through his thick blond hair. "It's been the same way since high school."

"I feel it necessary to point out that you both spent the better part of the last decade away from this town. Neither one of you know everything that went on with Brynn or with me during that time."

Finn and Parker both had issues with their respective fathers while growing up and had left their hometown for college without looking back. Nick had done the same thing—or at least that had been his plan until his brother died. His two friends hadn't returned to Starlight until this past summer to attend Daniel's funeral. It had been easy to slip back into friendship, but there was no denying all of them had changed in the intervening years.

"Besides, I'm keeping our pact even if I'm the only man standing." He ignored how foolish the words sounded, as if anything could block his feelings for Brynn.

"It's not a pact if there's only one person upholding it," Finn pointed out. He straightened the cuffs of his crisp white button-down. Although Finn had taken over the running of the bank his family owned in Starlight, like Parker, he still dressed the part of a big-city executive with tailored suits and expensive Italian loafers.

But there was no denying his dedication to the town. In the same way, Parker had partnered with Starlight's most accomplished attorney, who'd been waiting for the right moment to transition out of his practice.

Nick couldn't help but feel a tiny bit jealous of his friends. They'd gotten to leave town, experience the world and return on their own terms. It might not have felt like it to them when they first arrived back, but he'd never had the choice to make something of himself outside of who people knew him to be.

He'd changed, and it was more than the uniform he wore or the outward appearance of honor. His role in town wasn't just a job to him, although it had started that way when he'd first come back and joined the department.

He'd come to care, more than he ever thought possible, about the town, its history and future. It got under his skin that his friends didn't think he was capable of taking care of Remi.

Never mind that he would have said the same thing back in the day. "I'm not telling Brynn anything. She's got enough to deal with, and I won't be a complication she doesn't need. What she does need is for me to be her friend. She needs support, and I'm going to give her that."

"You have a second chance with her," Finn urged. "Baby or no."

"No." Nick crossed his arms over his chest and refused to think about what it had felt like to kiss Brynn. The taste of her and her inherent softness. He wouldn't let his own selfish desires eclipse his intention to help her.

His two friends shared a look. "What can we do?" Parker asked after a moment.

He stared at them.

"To help with the baby," Finn clarified.

"To help with whatever you need," Parker added around a bite of sandwich. "We may not agree, but we're here for you."

The band choking his gut eased and he blew out an unsteady breath. "You're probably right about me," he admitted. "I got certified as a foster parent so I could help older kids. I'm unqualified to have a baby in my care."

"So are most new parents." Parker shrugged. "We came in here to give you grief."

"Mainly to see how you'd react," Finn said. "This new, responsible, town golden boy Nick takes some getting used to. We remember the Nick who didn't give a care about anything or anyone."

"A test?" Nick rolled his eyes. "You two weren't the only ones who grew up over the past ten years. I know that a baby is different. You should have seen Brynn's face when she thought they were going to take Remi away from Starlight, even for a few weeks. I owe her after how I treated her in high school."

"She might disagree," Finn said quietly. "Have you talked to her about what happened back then?"

"There's nothing to talk about." Nick couldn't imagine revisiting that time or the pain he'd caused both of them with his selfishness. "I'm going to do my best with Remi until Francesca returns or until Brynn's foster application is approved. She shouldn't be punished for the fact that her father was a jerk."

"You're not alone," Parker reminded him. "You've got Brynn and you've got us. Even Mara was charmed by that little girl, and she's a hard sell when it comes to small creatures."

"But you should still," Finn said with a raised brow, "talk to Brynn about your feelings."

"Hard pass," Nick muttered. "I can't even believe you spoke the words *talk about your feelings*. Hello, Pot. This is Kettle calling."

Finn grinned. "What can I say? I'm a changed man. The love of an amazing woman will do that to you."

"Pass me a barf bag," Nick told his friend, ignoring the stab of jealousy piercing his chest.

"When do we get to meet her?" Parker asked with a grin.

"Brynn asked if I'd bring her to the holiday concert at the mill tonight."

"She's doing a hell of a job with marketing the events. Josh said they've exceeded projections for revenue the past two months and the holiday season is going to be even bigger than expected."

While Parker and his brother, Josh, had worked on getting the mill up and running together, Parker had turned his attention to establishing his law practice in Starlight once they'd had the grand opening. Josh still focused on his construction company but also retained his ownership in the mill.

"It's given her a shot in the arm of confidence. I hope taking on a baby won't deter that."

"You know Josh will give her a flexible schedule. She's not alone and neither are you."

Finn leaned in. "Is this the part where we talk about the fact that Kaitlin and Mara haven't given up on finding Mr. Right for Brynn?"

"She won't have time for dating," Nick observed. "Not with Remi in the picture."

"Are you sure about that?" his friend asked.

"I'm sure." In truth, Nick wasn't sure at all. He assumed Remi's arrival would put everything else on the back burner, but he hadn't actually discussed Brynn's love life with her.

"My wife is determined that Brynn gets another chance at love." Parker popped the final bite of sandwich into his mouth and balled up the paper it had been wrapped in. "When Mara sets her mind on something, look out, world."

A knock sounded at his office door, and Marianne peeked her head in, looking like she wished she'd been a fly on the wall for the past twenty minutes. "Your appointment is here."

"Lunch break is over," Nick announced, tossing the sandwich wrapper into the trash can next to his desk. This conversation had unsettled him more than he cared to admit.

His two friends did the same. "We'll see you tonight," Finn told him. "I don't want to make you all squeamish with talk of emotions or friendship, but know we've got your back."

Parker nodded. "Always."

Anxiety skittered down Brynn's spine as she watched the Starlight residents filing into the open space in the center of the mill. Skittered like a million arachnids tap dancing along her nerve endings. She couldn't tell which she was more nervous about—the first in a series of weekly holiday performances she'd arranged or the thought of Nick bringing baby Remi to the mill and the knowledge of Brynn's plan to adopt her late husband's illegitimate child becoming public.

It was bound to happen sooner or later, and with how small towns worked, she understood that she needed to control the narrative before the gossips got a hold of it.

She'd met her mom early that morning, before Whitney's daily water aerobics class at the community center's indoor pool.

Brynn's mom had taken the news about as well as Brynn expected. She'd stomped around the small kitchen, railing about Brynn's life being dictated by mistakes and Daniel topping the list even after his death.

Then she'd predictably gone down the path of how the news would affect her and the nosy neighbors she'd have to deal with and the judgment she was sure to get from people she counted as friends in the community.

Not once in her ten-minute tirade had Whitney asked about Brynn or Tyler and how they were dealing with this latest revelation of a husband and father's betrayal.

Par for the course, but it still hurt. Brynn wished she could turn that part of herself off. The part that still cared about her mother's disappointment in her.

As she'd done a decade earlier, she would put on her blinders and move forward. Tyler and Remi were her priorities, and she could take comfort in the fact that she was stronger now. She had friends, a support system and proof that she was a survivor.

The trick now was switching from survival mode to flourishing in life.

She waved to Mara, who walked in with Parker, her daughter, Evie, as well as Josh and his daughter, Anna.

Josh, who was both a few inches taller and broader than his older brother Parker, gave her two big thumbs-up, and pride chased away some of her nervous energy.

The interior of the mill had been transformed into a winter wonderland, with strands of twinkling lights, ribbons and fresh greenery from a local nursery. Although the temperature was cold, lines had formed at the three different food trucks parked in front of the main building.

She'd checked and double-checked with Martin Nielsen, the director of the high school honor choir. He displayed a calm disposition and had been the choir and theater director at the school since Brynn was a student there. He'd always encouraged her to participate in extracurricular activities, but she'd been too shy to do anything more than volunteer for the stage crew.

She was about to go look into things with the various shop owners when she caught sight of Nick walking toward the entrance from the parking lot, Remi's infant seat hooked on one arm. From where she stood, it was easy to watch people staring at Nick. If he felt the attention, he did a great job of ignoring it.

Brynn had kept herself mostly hidden. She preferred to work behind the scenes normally, but tonight in particular she relished her role out of the spotlight.

Ignoring her anxiety, she moved toward Nick. The crowd in front of her seemed to part as if people could sense her focus like a palpable force. A few called out greetings, but most simply watched her, curiosity burning in their gazes.

She didn't relish the thought of being the topic of conversation throughout every holiday event scheduled in Starlight over the next few weeks. As much as she knew she shouldn't rely on him, having Nick in this with her did make the whole situation a bit easier.

"Thanks for bringing her," she said, her heart filling as she gazed down at Remi, who was sucking on her pacifier. Nick had covered her with a blanket and put a knit cap on her head so only her face was visible. "How was today?"

"Mom said she slept and ate like a champ. She really is an easy baby."

"You better knock on wood," she told him with a laugh. "Tyler is getting dessert with friends. Let's bring her to my office until the show starts. I told him I'd meet him in front of the stage. He's curious as to what Remi's favorite song will be."

"Can a five-month-old baby have that kind of preference?"

She flashed a smile, still aware of the myriad of gazes on them. "I have no idea."

"Everyone is watching," Nick murmured, his thick brows drawing together. "I know you don't like to be scrutinized. I'd like to tell them to—"

"It's okay." She placed a hand on his arm, squeezing gently. "I'm learning not to care what other people think. It's a lesson I wish I'd mastered a long time ago."

He looked like he wanted to say something more but only nodded and followed her as she made her way through the people gathered.

"Stop glaring," she commanded, glancing over her shoulder. "People are starting to look more afraid than curious."

"Good," he muttered. "Maybe that will stop them from asking stupid questions."

Brynn appreciated the sentiment even if she knew he couldn't stop the curiosity. She unlocked the door that led to the mill's private rooms. At the moment, Josh was basing his construction business out of the location, so in addition to her small office, there were several rooms dedicated to his general contracting company.

Wanting the spirit of the holidays to permeate every inch of the mill, she'd decorated with fresh wreaths and more bows and greenery, so the sweet smell of pine filled the air.

She led Nick into her office and flipped on the

light. He set the infant carrier on the ground, and she immediately bent to unbuckle the baby.

"Hello, sweet girl," she said, kissing Remi's soft forehead. "I missed you today. What a pretty outfit." She'd dropped off the red velvet dress to Nick's mom, along with a dozen other pieces of clothing she'd bought. She knew Francesca could return, and nothing was certain, but Brynn already felt like the baby belonged to her. "I want to hear all about your adventures."

Remi gurgled in response, then grinned as the pacifier dropped into her lap. "Did you really? And then what did she say?" Brynn asked, lifting the girl into her arms.

"Um…did you actually understand her babbling?" Nick asked, sounding astonished.

Brynn shook her head as she held the baby close. "I used to talk to Tyler the same way. For some reason, it felt like asking him questions made him more vocal."

"You're a regular Dr. Spock," Nick murmured.

She chuckled. "What do you know about Dr. Spock?"

"My mom left the book on my nightstand. I'm not sure she took into consideration that between my normal work schedule, the extra shifts I volunteer for the weeks leading up to Christmas and taking care of a baby, my only choice might be winging it."

"I'm sorry," Brynn said automatically. "I know this is a lot for you and you volunteered because—"

"Because I wanted to help." He reached out a finger and pressed it to her lips. She felt the touch all the way to her toes. "There's nothing you need to apologize for, Brynn. Ever."

"I'm not perfect, Nick."

"Damn close," he whispered, then looked genuinely surprised when she narrowed her eyes. "Um… that was a compliment."

"I've made mistakes," she said, shifting the baby to her other arm and popping the pacifier into Remi's mouth. "I can be selfish and petty. A lot of times I make decisions based on avoiding conflict instead of taking a stand. My marriage was a perfect example of that."

"You can't blame yourself for anything that happened with Daniel."

"I can blame myself for being a doormat," she countered, then raised a hand when he would have protested. "I don't want to be on anyone's pedestal, either."

A muscle ticked in his jaw as he stepped closer. "What do you want?"

You, her body screamed. If only she had a roll of duct tape, she'd use it on her traitorous lady parts. Where the heck was a self-preservation instinct when she needed it?

"I want to be seen for who I am, flaws and all."

Before he could answer, she stepped around him.

"I need to get back out there before Tyler starts looking for me. Thank you, Nick. Thank you for everything."

to get what I needed out of the supply closet and run. I'll need to get back out there before Tyler turns

Chapter Nine

If ever Brynn needed a reminder that her life had turned out exactly how it was meant to, the holiday concert served that purpose.

Not only had she been surrounded by friends the moment she and Remi walked back into the throng of people, but Mara and Kaitlin had stayed at her side the entire night. They were like two sentry guards, ready to attack if anyone dared come forward to give her grief for wanting to take in the baby her late husband had fathered with one of his mistresses.

Tyler had bounced up to her before the start of the concert, seemingly unaware people might have a reason to frown on her decision to keep Remi. He'd proudly introduced his two best friends to his new sister.

To Brynn's surprise, several parents she knew from the elementary school also approached to coo and fuss over the baby. Remi preened under the attention, offering charming baby smiles, then tucking her head against Brynn's shoulder when she felt shy. By the time the music started with "Santa Claus Is Comin' To Town," she felt far more relaxed than she had in a long time.

She purposely didn't look around to make eye contact with anyone who might not approve of her decision. Instead, the knowledge that she had a core group of people to support her bolstered her confidence. In addition to Mara and Kaitlin, Parker and Finn stayed close. She could feel Nick behind her even though she didn't turn around.

As the popular holiday songs and carols continued, she could sense the audience was totally enamored with the performance. Although the show was free, they were accepting donations to go toward a spring break trip for the honor choir. After three songs, Martin paused to introduce the soloists and give background on the choir, including a plug for donations.

Then Josh took the makeshift stage to thank everyone for coming and for the support of Dennison Mill. As Brynn had worked out with the business owners, he announced a calendar of daily discounts for the different shops and explained that the mill would be donating to various local charities as a thank-you to each group performing throughout the holiday season, including five-hundred dollars toward the choir's spring break trip.

Brynn smiled as the students on stage cheered and the crowd applauded. This was exactly the reaction she'd wanted. Part of her plan to make the Dennison Mill project a success was positioning them as a community partner.

"I'd also like to give a special shout-out to the person whose tireless work has made all of this holiday hoopla possible."

"Oh, no," Brynn whispered, starting to take a step away.

"You can't run away," Nick said, his breath warm against her ear. He placed a steadying hand on her lower back. "You've earned this."

Blood pounded in her head as Brynn listened to Josh's praise. She knew she was doing a good job, or at least trying her best. But Brynn wasn't used to being singled out in this manner.

If people weren't looking at her before, she was the center of attention now. Tyler stepped closer and even Remi seemed to notice, pausing as she sucked on her pacifier.

When Josh finished, the thunderous round of applause had tears pricking the backs of her eyes. Yet, she could also imagine the comments and questions that would come as she stood there holding a baby who didn't yet belong to her.

"Keep smiling," Mara told her, as if sensing her nerves.

Kaitlin wrapped an arm around Brynn's shoulder. "We're all so proud of you."

Brynn mouthed a thank-you to Josh and then the concert continued. She felt both proud and overwhelmed.

"Let me take her for a minute," Nick said when Remi began to squirm. Mara was watching as Parker danced with Evie and Anna, and Finn had wrapped his arms around Kaitlin, gently swaying to a holiday classic.

She forced herself to meet his gaze as he lifted the baby from her arms. "Everyone is going to be talking about me."

"Because you kicked butt here tonight."

"That's not the reason, and we both know it."

His gaze gentled and he quickly squeezed her fingers. Subtly, so no one watching would notice. "I thought you were done caring about what other people thought about you."

"I was at the moment we discussed it." She rolled her eyes. "I wish it were so easy to stay strong."

"I know," he said quietly, and the understanding in his tone was a bigger comfort than she could have guessed. "I also know you're not perfect. Remember, I was the one who watched you fling boogers across the room while we played video games."

"Oh. My. God. I never flung boogers." Brynn shoved him, but it was like trying to move a mountain. His strength reminded her he'd changed as much as she had over the years.

"If only we'd had camera phones back in the day."

At that moment, the choir began a rousing rendition of "All I Want for Christmas." Remi let out a squeal of delight, pumping her arms and legs.

Tyler grinned at the baby. "Is this one your favorite, Remi?" he asked in a singsong voice.

More squealing and toothless grins came from the girl.

Tyler smiled at Brynn. "I knew she'd tell us her favorite."

"Wow." Brynn placed a hand on her son's head. "You know her well, bud." She shared a look with Nick, who appeared as flabbergasted as she felt that Remi indeed seemed to have an opinion on a favorite Christmas song.

The baby giggled as Nick began to sing along with the choir, sliding back and forth as he danced with her.

Tyler and his friends sang, too, along with Anna and Evie.

Brynn's breath caught because she was happy in a way she hadn't been for as long as she could remember. She knew things wouldn't always feel as easy as they did at this moment. The push and pull of disappointment and joy were familiar companions to her, both of them a comfort in their own way.

But she'd also been through enough to grasp on to pure happiness when it offered itself up like the bloom of a Christmas cactus, a wonderful surprise after so many months of lying dormant. Instead of worrying about what tomorrow might bring, she began to sing along, letting the words of the song remind her of the magic of the season.

The clock on the nightstand read 4:30 a.m. when Nick woke Monday morning to the sound of his cell phone's insistent ringing.

Groggy with sleep, he picked up the device, his gut clenching when he read the name of the incoming caller.

"Barrett," he said, as he accepted the call from Starlight's fire chief. "What happened?"

"She's okay," Kellen Barrett answered, then coughed as if he'd inhaled smoke. "They're both okay, Nick."

Nick's mind raced with the possibilities of what the other man wasn't telling him. "Who?" he demanded. "What the hell is going on, Chief?"

"There was a fire at Brynn Hale's house tonight. We think it started when a faulty strand of lights overloaded an electrical socket."

Nick let out a stream of curses so colorful it would have made a hardened sailor blush.

"I'm going to need you to keep it together," Kel said on a sigh. "You two are close—or whatever you'd call it—so I thought you'd want to know."

"Yeah." Nick was out of the bed and pulling on a pair of jeans. "I'll get over there as soon as I can. You're sure Brynn and Tyler—"

"Shell-shocked but fine. The fire spread to the kitchen before we could contain it, so the main floor of the house is a mess, but no one was hurt."

"Thanks for the call, Kel," Nick said. "I'm on my way."

He grabbed a sweatshirt from the chair next to his dresser and was halfway down the hall when he realized he couldn't go anywhere without Remi.

He blew out a shaky breath and thumped his fist against his forehead. In his panic over Brynn, he'd almost forgotten the baby in his care.

What kind of an idiot forgot a baby?

Brynn would have his head if he disturbed the girl's sleep, so he punched in Finn's number. He and Kaitlin lived closer to town than Parker, so they could be at Nick's house sooner.

His friend picked up on the third ring, sounding as sleepy as Nick had felt a few minutes earlier. Like Nick, Finn woke up immediately as he explained the situation in succinct sentences. They disconnected, and Nick paced the length of his first floor, imagining the fear that Brynn and Tyler must have felt to wake up to their house in flames. His heart twisted as a thousand horrible might-have-beens raced through his mind.

He tried calling her twice, but both times it went straight to voice mail. For all he knew, her phone was still inside the house. Kel wouldn't lie about her being fine, but Nick would only feel secure when he saw her for himself.

It felt like hours before he heard Finn's car pull up to his house, but in reality only eight minutes had passed.

Finn and Kaitlin rushed toward the front of the house as Nick opened the door. "I'll try to be back before she wakes up. In case I'm not, there's formula in the fridge, and I put the dry rice cereal she has for breakfast in a bowl on the counter. Just add water to that and heat the bottle—"

"I've got it," Kaitlin interrupted, placing a hand on Nick's arm. "Go."

With a terse nod, he headed for the garage.

"Give us any updates you can," Finn called after him.

"Take care of her," Kaitlin added.

With my life, he promised silently.

The few minutes it took to get to her house felt like an eternity. He drummed his fingers on the steering wheel and glanced at his phone every few seconds. Maybe a text would come through. Another call. He needed to hear her voice.

As he drove through Starlight's darkened streets, Nick noticed how many houses had left their lights on overnight. Plastic holiday figures still glowed in the night, and he could see a number of Christmas trees shining from front windows. He'd need to talk to Kel about posting to the town's social media accounts about holiday-decorating safety.

As he rounded the corner to the block on Maple Lane where Brynn lived, the glow of a fire truck's lights flashed ahead of him. His heart stuttered at the sight of an ambulance parked at the curb. He parked directly behind the emergency vehicle, then jumped out of the truck.

"Sir?" A young man, who Nick didn't recognize, wearing a firefighter's uniform approached him. "You can't be—"

"It's fine, Jacob. Chief Dunlap belongs here."

The firefighter enthusiastically nodded. "Sorry, Chief."

Nick nodded to the young man and then turned his attention to Kel. "Where is she?"

"Tyler wanted to check out the control panel on the ladder truck. They're on the far side."

Nick stared at the house as he moved past the two firefighters. It looked normal from the exterior, other than the firefighters moving in and out.

He walked around the front of the fire truck, his

heart hammering, then stopped in his tracks. Brynn stood next to the truck with a blanket wrapped around her shoulders. Her hair was tucked behind her ears and she had a gray smudge of soot across one cheek. And she was smiling. Not a fake stiff grin like she was struggling to hold it together.

He took another step forward and saw Tyler flipping instrument levers while two firefighters stood nearby.

"Brynn."

She turned at the sound of his voice and for a brief instant the emotion that appeared in her gaze overwhelmed him. He saw fear and vulnerability and she swiped at the corner of one eye even as she forced a smile back into place.

"I'm okay," she whispered.

He walked forward, laughing that he'd thought it would be enough to see that she was fine and hear her voice. He needed more. He needed to—

She met him halfway. The blanket fell to the ground as he gathered her close. Once again, she fit perfectly in his arms.

"You're okay," he said into her hair, which smelled like smoke.

"I just said that," she told him with a shaky laugh.

He leaned back, cupping her hand between his palms. "Don't scare me again."

He saw her throat work as she swallowed. "I woke up and smelled smoke. It was heavy, Nick,

crew for getting here so quickly. Things could have been a lot worse."

"Thanks," Tyler dutifully told the chief.

"My pleasure, son." Kel led the boy around the truck, the word *son* reverberating through Nick's chest.

Tyler had no father.

"Have you talked to your mom yet?" He bent his knees so he was at eye level with Brynn.

She shook her head.

"I know you don't want to move back in that house."

"What choice do I have?"

"Mara and Kaitlin—"

"Have lives of their own. I won't be a burden to them."

"Neither of them would consider you a burden."

"We'll be fine at my mom's," she insisted even as she cringed. "Hopefully Josh will have a crew over here quickly. Maybe we'll be back in by Christmas?"

"Stay with me," he said on a rush of breath.

Her lips parted. "You don't mean that."

He shouldn't make the offer. Not with how being near Brynn affected him. It was hard enough planning to see her regularly because of Remi. Having her under his roof would be like slow torture. Reminding him of all the things he didn't—couldn't—have in his life.

"I do," he said because clearly he had an emotional death wish. "I have the extra rooms and it will be good for Remi. You won't have to go back and forth between my house and yours to see her. Tyler would love it."

She shook her head. "I'm not sure, Nick. What will people think?"

"Who cares? It's the right thing." Now that the idea had taken root, he couldn't seem to shake it. He knew this rediscovered closeness with Brynn would most likely stop when her foster application went through. The built-in end date made the whole thing almost irresistible. "No one can deny the connection Tyler has with Remi but visiting a baby for an hour or so is different than having one move into your house. This will get him used to the day-to-day business of sharing you and his home in a place that's neutral for him."

"You sound like a counselor." The barest glimmer of a smile played around the edges of her mouth. "When did you get so smart, Chief Dunlap?"

"I was born this way. You never noticed before now because you were too dazzled by my good looks."

Her eyes went wide for a moment, and he wondered if he'd overstepped with the teasing. "I was dazzled by you. That part is true." She rolled her eyes. "But I guarantee you didn't show this kind of insight when we were younger."

He should make some funny comment back to

her, keep the moment light. Instead, he let his gaze lower to her mouth as he took the soft ends of her hair between his fingers. "I might not have messed things up so badly if I had."

She drew in a sharp breath and he stepped away. This was not the time to spook her. "Come on, Brynn," he coaxed. "We both know it's not going to be good for anyone if you stay with your mom."

"She doesn't even want to meet Remi," Brynn told him, her full lips pressing into a thin line.

"Her loss," he said quietly. "All along it's been her loss. Say yes. Please."

She shifted and looked to where Tyler had disappeared with Kel. Without turning back to Nick, she nodded. "Yes," she said finally. "Thank you for the offer. I appreciate it and promise we won't disrupt your life." Now she did turn to him. "Very much anyway," she added with a smile.

"Easy as pie," he said, ignoring the fact that his heart was beating as fast as if he'd just finished running a marathon.

Chapter Ten

"It's no big deal," Nick told Remi later that morning. "She's a friend, and I'm doing her a favor. Nothing more."

The baby hopped up and down in the jumping seat he'd affixed in a doorway. She chewed on her fist, drool pooling around her chubby fingers.

"No one believes me," he continued, taking her silence for agreement. "This isn't about my feelings for Brynn. I'd make the offer for anyone."

Remi gurgled and bounced with enthusiasm.

"Okay, maybe not for Cyndi Jennings." He stared at the baby, hands on hips. "When the candle burned down her living room, I wasn't about to offer to move her into my house. She kept telling me how limber she was because of her gymnast history."

When the baby continued to bounce, her attention now focused on the ceiling, Nick let out a sigh. He'd thought it strange when Brynn talked to Remi like she could understand, but he found himself having one-sided conversations more often than not.

Remi might not be able to respond with words, but it still felt like she was a good listener.

Voices at the front of his house had him moving toward the door. Teddy barked and trotted along at his side. "Best behavior," he warned the dog. "We're both going to be on our best behavior while they're here."

The black Lab whined low in his throat.

"No matter how hard it is for either of us."

He opened the door as Kaitlin walked up the porch steps followed by Tyler holding a pillow tight between his arms and carrying a backpack that looked like it weighed about as much as he did.

"Can I help?"

"Is Remi awake or napping?" Tyler asked, scratching Teddy's soft head.

"In her jumper seat in the kitchen. If you want to go check on her, I'll help your mom unload the car."

"There's not much," Kaitlin told him. "She only packed enough for a few days. I think she's still hoping that Josh will perform some renovation miracle."

"If anyone can, it would be Josh, but I doubt it."

"It was nice of you to let her stay here." Kaitlin looked over her shoulder. "Finn and I would have been happy to have them but…"

"She has a hard time accepting help." Nick sighed. "I've known her long enough that I could get away with bullying her into it."

"I doubt you bullied her," Kaitlin said with a laugh.

"I think Remi being here sealed the deal. You can put the suitcases at the bottom of the staircase. I'll get the rest."

She nodded but her brows drew together as if she wanted to say more. Whatever it was, Nick didn't want to hear it, so he jogged down the front walk to Brynn's compact Toyota.

The sun was just rising, and a light wind had picked up, reminding him that although it didn't snow often in this part of the state, winter was fully on its way.

"You travel light," he said, offering her a smile, which he noticed she didn't return.

"I ruined it." She tugged her lower lip between her front teeth. "A few weeks before Christmas and I've ruined everything."

The pain in her voice made his heart hurt. He grasped her arms and squeezed. "Nothing is ruined, Brynn."

"Tyler's already been through so much this year and now we're going to be displaced for Christmas."

She tried to laugh but it came out sounding more like a sob. "Imagine the years of therapy he's going to need to process all of this. I'm the worst moth—"

"Don't say that." He placed a finger to her mouth. "You're a fantastic mom. Yes, he's had trauma, but you're seeing him through it. If he needs counseling when he's older, you'll support him through that, as well. Hell, I see enough people in my job that could use someone to talk to. There's no shame."

She swiped at her cheeks. "I'd never make him feel ashamed. Unfortunately, I'm another story."

He could see the dark circles under her eyes and the sharp pull of worry at the corners of her mouth. "You're exhausted, sweetheart."

"Great. On top everything else, I look like crap."

"I didn't say that." Nick let her go and picked up a duffel bag as she closed the trunk. "You're always beautiful. But a fire is upsetting for anyone. Let's go inside, have something to eat and then you and Tyler can get some rest."

"Nick."

"Yes?"

"You don't have to do that."

"What?"

"Call me beautiful." She strapped her purse to one shoulder and began to wheel her suitcase up the walk. "It's the second time you've made the comment in the past week. I've never been beautiful, and at this point in my life, I don't care. You don't have to try to placate me."

"I'm a lot of things," he told her, as he followed. "But I don't lie, and I won't blow sunshine up anyone's skirt. Even yours. I'm telling you you're beautiful because it's true, Brynn. Whether you choose to believe me is on you."

They got to the porch and he grabbed the suitcase's handle when she would have lifted it. "Let me get that. You and Tyler will be staying upstairs. I moved Remi to the sitting room so Ty can have the spare bedroom and she'll be across the hall. You'll have the master."

"I can't take your bedroom," she said, sounding shocked that he'd made the suggestion.

"It's already done." He entered the house and gave Teddy a quick scratch between the ears. "I've moved my things to the office on the first floor. It has a pullout couch."

"Nick, no."

"Mom, come and watch Remi jump," Tyler hollered from the kitchen.

"Go ahead," Nick said with a smile. "I'll bring the bags upstairs."

"Leave mine down here," she told him. "I don't mind the pullout."

Like hell he was going to put her on a lumpy sofa-bed mattress. Nick could sleep wherever, so the arrangement suited him fine.

"Mom!"

"Coming," she called. "We're not done with this discussion," she said to Nick's back.

She could discuss it until the cows came home. Nick wasn't going to change his mind. It took two trips to transfer all of the luggage upstairs. He deposited it in their respective bedrooms, replacing the pillow in the spare room with the one Tyler brought. He wished the boy had more things to make him feel at home.

He made his way back downstairs as Kaitlin was leaving.

"Thanks for your help," he told her. Her car was parked at the curb in front of Brynn's.

"If this doesn't work out, she's welcome with us." She gave him an expectant look. "I know Mara and Parker feel the same."

"She's fine here."

The blonde didn't look convinced. "Finn says you're in love with her," she said in a hushed tone. Her hand tightened on the doorknob.

"Finn talks too much," Nick grumbled. "Brynn and I are friends, and I haven't been a very good one. I'm making up for lost time."

"She needs someone who will put her first in his life." She studied Nick. "Mara and I still have a number of potential suitors in mind."

"Suitors?" Nick choked out a laugh to hide the irritation that flamed in his chest. "Is this the eighteenth century? I'm sure Brynn is plenty capable of finding herself a date if she wants one."

"She wants one." Kaitlin clearly wasn't going to argue the point. "We promised her twelve dates before Christmas."

"I heard," he muttered.

"She's been on two so far."

He wondered if the pretty blonde could hear his teeth grinding. "I know."

"We discussed the number of dates but not who she'd go out with. The point isn't for her to meet a dozen different men. I'll admit Mara and I hoped she'd meet a nice man and have multiple dates with him." Kaitlin leaned in closer like she was telling him a secret. "With her Mr. Right. Any ideas of whom that might be?"

Nick's breath stuttered to a halt in his lungs. He couldn't imagine Brynn's friends would think he'd make a good match. Not when Finn and Parker understood how badly he'd treated her in high school. And they knew about his vow regarding love. Dating and a moratorium on love didn't exactly go hand in hand.

"I'm not right for her." The words sounded rough as they rolled off his tongue.

"She's got a lot going on right now," Kaitlin said as if he hadn't spoken. "It would be nice if someone she trusted could help her enjoy the next few weeks. She deserves a special Christmas. She and Tyler both."

He nodded. "Yeah, they do." Maybe he wasn't perfect or right for her, but he'd vowed to himself to help her through this Christmas. Maybe the fact that her friend seemed to support the idea meant he wasn't so ill-fitted for the role, after all. At least temporarily. "I'll do my best."

Kaitlin gave him a slow smile. "That's all anyone can do."

Brynn stared at the ceiling of Nick's bedroom late that night, wishing she could fall asleep. She was afraid to nod off to dreams of Nick and then wake in the morning alone in his bed.

She was lying in Nick's bed. They'd argued about where she should sleep, but in the end, it had been Tyler who'd convinced her to give up the fight. As the boy's bedtime had drawn closer, he'd gotten an almost haunted look on his face. The same look she remembered from the weeks after Daniel's death. He'd taken her hand and asked how far her bedroom was from the one he was staying in.

The vulnerability in his eyes had torn her heart open all over again. She'd offered that he could sleep in the bed with her, but her sweet, brave son had insisted that he'd be fine in his own bed.

Nick had told the boy they were safe, and that Nick would be right there if anything happened or if Brynn, Tyler or Remi needed him. Tyler had listened intently and then let out a heavy sigh, his shoulders deflating as if they'd been carrying a heavy weight.

He'd put on a brave face when she picked him up from school earlier that afternoon to pack his bag and move what was salvageable from the family room. Tears had lodged in her throat as she'd taken in the damage from the soggy carpet to the smoke-stained furniture.

After meeting with the insurance agent, she'd spoken with Josh at the mill and he'd promised to start the restoration work as soon as possible and that his crew would make the house even better than it had been.

Better was good but with all of the changes pummeling them, Brynn could have done without updated appliances if it meant a little consistency in her world.

She threw back the covers and placed her feet on the thick rug that took up most of the floor. How in the world was she supposed to sleep with Nick's scent surrounding her all night? He'd told her the sheets were clean, but under the freshness of laundry detergent was his smell. She'd hung her clothes next to his in the closet, and it had taken a monumental effort to resist burying her face in his shirts.

Her body felt charged with electricity, and tonight was only the beginning.

No, she scolded herself. She would not freak out about Nick's smell or the way his laugh rumbled through her when he reacted to the jokes Tyler liked to tell.

But she appreciated being able to put Remi down for bed and then tuck in her son without having to get in her car and drive to a different house.

Nick had been right that being together would make them feel like a family. Remi was a great distraction for Tyler, a silver lining in the dark cloud of the fire damage. If only Brynn didn't notice how well Nick fit into their little family.

She straightened from the bed and slipped across the hall, quietly opening the door to Tyler's bedroom. Her son was sprawled across the mattress, the raggedy stuffed bear he'd packed clasped in his arms. Cleo had been his favorite lovey since he was a baby, although now the well-worn bear spent most of its time on the bookshelf of his bedroom.

Watching him sleep with Cleo tonight made Brynn nostalgic for the passage of time.

After shutting the door again, she went to check on Remi, who was also sleeping soundly. Then Brynn padded down the stairs and headed for the kitchen. Maybe a glass of milk would settle her nerves.

A light glowed from the partially open doorway of Nick's office. Her breath felt like it was coming out in strangled puffs as she moved toward it, drawn forward even though her rational mind warned she should run back up the stairs and not come out of the bedroom again until morning.

She knocked lightly and heard his answered greeting like she were listening from under a wave, his voice muffled from the pounding between her ears.

The office had an oversize cherry desk situated in front of the window and bookshelves lined one wall. On the wall to the other side of the door was the sofa bed. It looked to be at least full-size and not as uncomfortable as she'd imagined.

Nothing prepared her for the sight of a shirtless Nick propped against several fluffy pillows, a laptop open in front of him with a screen displaying...

"Is that the Lego website?" She stepped into the small room, still reeling from half-naked Nick but also confused and touched at what his browsing selection might mean.

"Tyler said the set he'd been working on in the family room melted." He shrugged, one big shoulder lifting, then lowering. Her attention focused on his body once again.

She'd seen Nick shirtless plenty of times when they were younger. The two of them would swim at the lake or run through the sprinklers in his family's backyard. And then in high school when it seemed like the entire football team took pains to parade around shirtless after practice.

But being with him in this cozy room reminded her how much had changed. Nick was a man in his prime and she was a late-twenties single mom of soon-to-be two kids with stretch marks on her breasts and hips.

If the rest of their differences didn't make clear why she was not a good match for Nick, the physical comparison—and there was no comparison—certainly would. Still, she wanted to beg him like some kind of obsessed fan girl to always walk around with no shirt while she was in the house.

"You don't have to do that," she said. "I have a plan for Christmas."

"I want to help," he answered simply. "Are you having trouble sleeping?"

She nodded. "On my way to the kitchen for a glass of milk."

He flipped back the covers to reveal a pair of loose gym shorts. "I can get it for you," he said, reaching for a T-shirt on the floor next to the bed.

"Don't."

The word came out sharper than she'd expected, and Nick paused and glanced at up her. His brows furrowed like her outburst didn't make sense, but his eyes darkened as if he could read her mind. "Don't go to the kitchen?"

"Don't put on the shirt."

She stepped closer. Her body hummed with awareness. She should back away, walk out of the office and shut the door behind her. What was she doing in here?

There were so many reasons this was a mistake, but at the moment Brynn didn't care about any of them. The sensations rolling through her were both unfamiliar and not. Worry and anxiety were constant companions, but they took a back seat to her visceral desire.

Would it be so bad to give in to it? Even for one night.

It had been so long since she'd done something for herself. Oh, her friends had talked to her about "self-care" after Daniel's death. She'd read plenty of articles that said a mom had to be good to herself in order to take care of her kids.

No at-home spa treatement or binge-worthy series in the world would compare to touching Nick.

He didn't speak as she took his hand and then sat down next to him, the thin mattress depressing under their combined weight. His chest rose and fell in ragged breaths and his gaze was intense on her, filled with so much need it was difficult to believe this was the same man who'd kept his distance from her this past decade.

With trembling fingers, she reached out and placed her hand on his shoulder. She traced a line along his collarbone, need pooling low in her belly at the heat and softness of his skin.

There was a scar just below his biceps, a tiny

mark she wasn't familiar with, which meant it had happened when he was an adult. She knew the dot of graphite from where Tommy Lencner had poked Nick with a pencil during a fifth-grade sword fight. One that had landed both of them with detention.

"What is it?" she whispered, fascinated by the raised skin.

"Knife wound," he said, his voice gruff.

She sucked in a breath.

"Not a big deal. It was my first year on the force and I was careless during a meth-lab bust. Surface wound. That's all, Brynn."

"Why didn't I know about this?"

What else didn't she know?

"Not many people did." He covered her hand with his. "I made a rookie mistake, so the fewer people who knew the better, as far as I was concerned."

"You could have been killed." She raised her gaze to his. "Any day you could be killed."

"That's not going to happen." He flashed a cocky smile. "I'm smarter now."

"Your job is dangerous." She flattened her palm on his chest. His heart raced. "You risk your life to serve the town."

He stiffened, as if a cold burst of air chased across the space between them. "Don't make me into something I'm not."

"What kind of something?"

He laughed without humor. "A hero."

"I don't need a hero." She licked her lips, swayed closer to him.

"What do you need, Brynn?"

Color stained his cheeks and a muscle ticked in his jaw, like it was taking every inch of strength he had to control his reaction to her.

Suddenly, Brynn was filled with the need to lose control and take Nick Dunlap along with her.

Without letting rational thought have a vote in the decision, she pressed her mouth to his.

Chapter Eleven

It only took a moment for the kiss to turn from exploring to demanding. Nick pulled her closer, almost into his lap, and her senses reeled as he moved his hands up and under her pajama top.

His rough palms on her heated skin were heaven. She opened for him as their kiss deepened.

He lowered himself back against the sheets, taking her with him. She straddled him as he continued to kiss her and wondered if she could ever get enough of this. He inched the baggy shirt up and over her head with one hand while the other unclasped her bra hook. Should she be alarmed at his dexterity? Even she couldn't unhook a bra that easily.

Brynn had the fleeting thought she should have

packed the lacy lingerie her friends had encouraged her to buy. Then they were skin to skin, and it didn't matter. Nothing mattered except this man and this moment.

"How are you this soft?" he whispered against her mouth, as his hands cupped the weight of her breasts. "So damn beautiful."

A denial bubbled into her mouth, but she swallowed it back. She might not have much experience with men, but she knew better than to reject a compliment, especially when it came from a man looking at her as if she were Christmas morning, the Fourth of July and his favorite team winning the Super Bowl all wrapped into one.

He lifted his head and covered one taut nipple with his mouth. Brynn moaned and braced her hands on either side of his broad shoulders. She was once again in jeopardy of spontaneously combusting from the desire swirling through her.

Nick seemed in no hurry to move things along. He took his sweet time giving attention to her sensitive breasts, and Brynn ground her hips into his.

She could feel how much he wanted her, and that knowledge inflamed her need. His hands settled on her hips, and his thumbs traced the edge of her pajama shorts. Goose bumps erupted along her skin as he continued to move higher on her upper thigh.

Just when she thought she couldn't hold herself upright from the pleasure, he flipped her onto her back, staring down at her like she was the most precious thing he'd ever seen.

But something else flashed in his gaze. A hint of trepidation, and she was terrified he'd stop touching her. Brynn wasn't sure if she'd make it through the night if he stopped now.

"I want you," she told him, lifting a palm to cup his rigid jaw. "I want this."

"Brynn." Her name on his lips sounded like a prayer. A plea.

"Please, Nick." She didn't care if she had to beg. There was nothing else that could fill the void inside her. Not at the moment. "I need—" she wrapped her arms around his neck and drew him down toward her "—you," she finished, then traced the tip of her tongue along the seam of his lips.

"Then I'm yours."

He slipped his hand into the waistband of her pajama shorts and panties, finding the spot that craved his touch. Her hips arched off the bed when he skimmed a finger along her center and bright spots of color flashed behind her closed eyes.

How was it possible he could make her feel so much with a simple touch?

"Open your eyes," he told her before sucking her earlobe into his mouth. He nuzzled her neck, then raised his head to gaze down at her as his fingers continued to work their magic. "I want to see you."

The look in his eyes was enough to push her over

the edge. She cried out, spiraling through the air like she was riding on a thousand points of light.

Nick bent his head again, whispering sweet things into her ear and placing gentle kisses along the column of her throat.

She waited for what came next, the feel of his body over hers, and swallowed back her shock when he moved to one side with a final kiss.

"We're not…" She sat up at the same time he did. "You didn't…"

He handed her top to her and shrugged into his shirt without making eye contact. "It's late," he said, his voice at once gruff and tender. "And you've had a traumatic day. I don't want to take advantage of you."

"What if you're not?" she said, pulling her shirt on over her head even as her body continued to tingle in the afterglow of her release. "What if I want—"

"I'm trying to be a friend," he said, running a hand through his hair.

A terrifying thought crawled into her still-fuzzy brain. "Oh, no." She shook her head. "Was that a pity…interlude?" Her cheeks flamed with embarrassment.

"No." Nick muttered a curse and then grabbed her hands, lifting them to his mouth. He grazed a kiss across her knuckles. "Of course not. Brynn, you have to know I want you. That watching you come apart in my arms was the best thing that's happened to me in forever. It was a dream come true."

She frowned. "Then why stop? I'm a big girl, Nick. I don't need you to worry about taking advantage of me. I'm capable of making my own decisions, and I know the difference between sex and love. Trust me. I know all about that."

"I'm not trying to make you mad." He squeezed her hands, then released her, standing to pace to the bookshelf. "I can't seem to do anything right where you're concerned."

Brynn couldn't help the laugh that escaped her lips. "You definitely did some things right."

He glanced at her, and some of the tension in his shoulders eased. "I want you, Brynn," he repeated. "I can barely control myself around you. That can't come as a surprise. But you had one hell of day. If we're going to be together, it will be the right time."

"Most of my life is based on timing that's been horribly wrong," she said quietly, straightening from the bed. "Why should this be any different?"

"Because you deserve better," he said tightly.

She wasn't sure whether she felt grateful or offended that he assumed he knew what she wanted or deserved. But she couldn't deny her body was way more relaxed than it had been when she'd knocked on his office door.

She should take that as a win at least.

"Good night, Nick," she said, knowing there was no point in arguing any more tonight.

"Sweet dreams," he told her, and she let herself out of his office.

By the end of the week, Nick felt like he might actually be going crazy with frustration. After her late-night trip to his office, Brynn hadn't spoken to him other than to discuss Remi's schedule or make meaningless small talk over dinner with Tyler.

He hated the distance that had emerged between them, when holding her in his arms had been the best feeling he'd had in ages. But he didn't regret not going further that night, despite how much his body continued to protest. As much as he wanted Brynn in his bed, his priority was being a good friend to her. To his mind, a decent guy wouldn't be selfish enough to be intimate with a woman who was traumatized by having half her house go up in flames.

He knew she'd met with Josh and his crew. According to the bits she'd told him, they were going to begin the project early next week and Josh hoped to have her back home by Christmas Eve. Nick found it hard to believe they could accomplish so much so quickly, and he'd been looking forward to waking up to watch Tyler open his presents on Christmas morning.

But it was important to Brynn that Tyler spend

the night before Christmas in his own bed and Nick would be a supportive friend, even if it killed him.

He walked into Trophy Room at five o'clock on Friday, forcing smiles for the locals who greeted him by name. Jordan Schaeffer, the bar's former-NFL-playing owner, waved from behind the bar, which was currently lined with customers. Nick knew it would only get more crowded as the night wore on, but he'd be long gone.

In fact, he didn't even want to be there at the moment, but Brynn was hosting some sort of annual cookie-baking party at his house. Kaitlin, Mara, Evie and Anna, along with Mara's aunt, his mom and two of her book-club friends were currently gathered in his kitchen.

Kaitlin and Mara had both offered to have the gathering at their houses, but he'd insisted Brynn invite everyone to his place. She'd put on such a brave face about the damage and the challenge of reconstruction, but the change in plans for her annual event had seemed to affect her like a physical blow.

He would not have her losing it over a few dozen cookies.

He headed for the table at the back, where Finn, Parker and Josh were waiting.

"I thought you'd be home rolling out fondant," Josh said with a laugh, moving over to make room for Nick.

The rest of them stared at the single dad, and

Nick was gratified to see his confusion was mirrored on his friends' faces. "What the hell is fondant?" Finn asked after a moment.

"Icing," Josh said, frowning. "You use it to decorate cakes and cookies."

Parker looked even more befuddled at his brother's familiarity with the details of pastry decorating. "Why do you know that?"

"Give me a break," Josh muttered. "Anna likes baking shows, and I watch with her. It's not like the man-card police are going to hunt me down for discussing the virtues of fondant or buttercream."

"There's more than one type of icing?" Nick grabbed a wing from the basket in the center of the table. "I thought it was all frosting."

They all turned as the waitress approached the table.

"The usual?" she asked, placing a cardboard coaster down in front of Nick.

"Please," he answered. "Jocelyn, have you heard of fondant?"

"It's the icing that tastes like crap, right?" She wrinkled her nose. "I like the spreadable stuff better."

Josh nodded. "Buttercream."

"Sure," Jocelyn agreed, then walked away.

"Do you wear a ruffled apron?" Parker asked his younger brother with a laugh.

Without hesitation, Josh flipped a one-fingered

salute. "Mara texted me the pic of you with a bubble mask when you did the spa night with Evie. Don't make me post it on the town Instagram account."

"I don't know anything about a bubble mask." Finn shook his head. "But does the fact that we're having a conversation that involves televised baking shows and spa nights mean we're officially lame?"

"I'm not lame," Nick protested, then thanked Jocelyn when she brought his beer to the table.

"You have dried spit-up on your shoulder," Josh told him.

"Fine." Nick took a long drink of beer to avoid checking his sweater. "I guess I'm lame along with the rest of you all."

"How's it going with your full house?" Finn asked, as he grabbed a wing and dipped it in blue cheese dressing. In addition to the basket of wings, they had a bowl of smoked cheese dip and the best jalapeño poppers Nick had ever tasted. Trophy Room was a throwback as far as decor, with its paneled walls and neon beer signs, but Jordan had hired a classically trained chef to update the bar's menu after he took over. She focused on classic bar food with a twist, so the wings were basted in a sesame soy glaze and a simple cheese dip had layers of flavors that even a big-city food snob would appreciate.

The bar had earned a reputation for serving the best selection of regional brews outside of Seattle and offering the most scrumptious menu items to go with them.

Nick normally wouldn't walk into the place on weekends, when tourists and visitors swarmed the valley. Despite the crowds, Jordan still managed to attract plenty of locals, so Nick always knew at least half the patrons by name.

"It's fine," he said, keeping his tone casual, almost flippant. "I like having the help with Remi at night. Makes me feel less like I'm going to make some kind of colossal mistake on my own."

"I think he was asking about Brynn." Parker raised a brow. "How's it going being so close to her again?"

"Fine," Nick repeated.

"That's the third time you've said *fine* since you sat down," Josh pointed out, none too helpfully. "You're not very convincing."

"What do you expect?"

The three men stared at him so long that he felt a bead of sweat drip down between his shoulder blades.

"I'm not going to have a relationship with her."

"Why are you being so stubborn?" Finn demanded. "Kaitlin and Mara are determined to find a man for Brynn, and we all know you never got over her."

"I was friends with her dead husband." Nick

shook his head. "Hell, I set them up in the first place."

"In high school," Parker reminded him. "A lot has changed since then."

Josh nodded and then waved a hand between Finn and Parker. "These two yahoos were gone for most of that time, but I've been here. I can vouch you were nothing but respectful toward Daniel and Brynn's marriage. I don't think anyone outside of your close circle of friends even knew you had feelings for her."

"Because it wasn't my place to have feelings for her." Nick took another long drink of beer. "I lost that right when I hurt her."

"You're different now," Finn said quietly.

"In a lot of ways," Nick agreed. "But I don't do relationships."

"You haven't done relationships," Parker corrected. "That doesn't mean you're incapable of it."

Josh chuckled and elbowed his brother. "If this one can take the plunge, I'd bet money anyone could."

"What about you?" Nick pointed a chicken wing in Josh's direction. "I'm not the only one who's single at this table. Maybe we could work on matchmaking for you, and I could get a damn break around here."

Josh sighed. "I'd love to find a nice, even-tempered woman to date."

"That sounds boring as hell," Finn said on a choked laugh.

"I've had the exciting whirlwind," Josh responded. "It didn't work out so well for me. Boring is right up my alley."

Nick hadn't known Josh's ex-wife well but he didn't think much of her. After a swift courtship and quickie wedding in Las Vegas, Josh and his bride had returned to Starlight, but as far as Nick could tell, Jenn had never been happy. The timing of their separation had been particularly brutal. Jenn left town shortly after their daughter, Anna, who was not even in kindergarten, had been diagnosed with cancer, leaving Josh on his own to handle the girl's treatments, as well as try to explain the breakup of their family.

Josh didn't talk much about the past, but it had been a dark time, and he deserved to find a good woman as much as Brynn did a good man.

"Boring is underrated," Parker agreed. "I never thought I could be entertained watching princess movies, but an evening on the couch with Mara and Evie beats a late night out at the bar any day."

Nick felt irritation prick his skin. He knew exactly what Parker was talking about and it annoyed the hell out of him. He'd ordered a Lego set from the internet and couldn't wait to put it together with Tyler when it arrived. What kind of grown-ass man was excited about overpriced plastic toys?

"Maybe you should date Brynn," he muttered to Josh.

"Because she's boring?" the other man asked with a frown.

"Hell, no, she's not boring." Nick wiped his fingers on a napkin and focused his gaze on his beer. "But she's nice, even-tempered and damn near perfect."

Josh shifted closer. "And you're okay with me asking her out?"

Nick ground his teeth. He opened his mouth to give his blessing, but the words refused to pass his lips. He should encourage the match. Kaitlin had told him that she and Mara weren't giving up on their stupid plan for twelve dates. Josh had been through the wringer with his divorce. Brynn's marriage had left her with far too many emotional scars. Maybe they'd be the perfect salve for each other.

The thought made Nick want to puke.

"No," he breathed out finally, then finished the rest of his beer. "Not even a little."

Finn patted him on the back. "Nice to see you can pull your head out for a few seconds. We can build on that."

"I don't deserve her," he said, needing his friends to understand. "She's too good for me."

"Duh." Parker threw up his hands. "You just hit on the magic, buddy. We're with these amazing women who are so far above us and somehow they love us anyway. Here's a little secret…" He leaned across the table. "You're a fool if you don't take the opportunity."

"I'll think about it," he said through clenched teeth. "But can you all stop Dear Abby-ing my life for a few minutes so I can enjoy the wings in peace."

"Speaking of peace…" Finn made a face. "Or more likely a disturbance in the peace… Ella gets to town tomorrow. I mentioned Remi to her and she's up for nannying for a few weeks until she figures out her next steps."

Finn's younger sister, Ella, had been a wild child back in the day. She hadn't been on Nick's radar much, since she was a couple years younger. She'd gone out of her way to antagonize their rigid father, especially after their mom died while the kids were in high school. She'd left Starlight and gone to school to become a nurse.

Nick knew from Finn that she'd spent the past several years all over the globe as a travel nurse.

"How long has it been since you've seen her?" Parker asked gently.

"Too long." Finn's mouth pressed into a thin line. "She had a layover in San Fran a couple of years ago, so I flew down for lunch. I still don't understand why she's coming back right now. She'd always wanted to stay as far away from Starlight as possible."

"I never understood you people being so determined to leave this town behind," Josh said around a bite of popper. "I couldn't imagine living anywhere else."

Nick could. He'd had the same driving need to escape the confines of small-town life and his role in it that his friends did. The need had been even stronger once Brynn and Daniel married. Out of sight, out of mind and all that.

Now he wondered if returning to Starlight contributed to his commitment issues. How was he supposed to risk hurting another woman with the regular reminder of what his selfishness had done to Brynn?

It was a big part of why he'd stopped before things had gone too far with her. Too far when he knew they weren't meant to be.

"Tell her to call me when she's ready to meet Remi." He nodded at Finn. "My mom has been uncharacteristically great in this situation, but I can see that it tires her out."

"Kids are exhausting," Josh said with a laugh. "It's why they're made so cute."

Chapter Twelve

"This is irregular to say the least."

Brynn swallowed and gave Jennifer her brightest smile. "Nick and I have been friends since we were kids, and I appreciate that he's letting Tyler and me stay here. It's unconventional, but on the plus side, Remi is getting to know both me and her new brother more than she would have if we'd been only able to visit. When she's part of our family—"

"Nothing has been approved yet," Jennifer reminded her gently.

"But there's been no word from Francesca?" Nick prompted.

The social worker's mouth thinned as she shook her head. "Not yet."

A sliver of worry sliced through Brynn's chest. "Do you think she might return to claim Remi?" Brynn had set her mind and her heart on the idea that Remi would become her daughter.

She had so much love to give.

"She still has time before her parental rights are permanently terminated."

"She abandoned her baby." The note of panic must have been clear in Brynn's tone because Nick shifted closer to her on the sofa so he could cover her hand with his. Her gaze strayed to the baby, who was contentedly sucking on her pacifier in the social worker's arms.

"The law is clear that the priority needs to be re-unification with the biological parent. We discussed that in our first meeting."

"Yes, but…" Brynn trailed off. Of course, she'd heard the social worker's words, but she hadn't been able to process them through her shock. A thousand regrets rushed through her, and she suddenly felt like the most foolish mother that ever lived. What if Francesca returned? That would be enough of a blow, but what if the other woman was unwilling to forge a relationship between Tyler and his sister?

The boy had dealt with so much loss. They might have taken things slower, but Francesca leaving the baby with Brynn had given her no choice. He'd already formed a bond with his sister. Brynn refused to consider the possibility he might lose that, too.

"We'll cross that bridge if we come to it." Nick squeezed her hand. "We need to focus on Remi being safe and loved now. Brynn's reconstruction is on-track according to the contractor, so our living arrangement is only until Christmas. You can see the baby is thriving, Jennifer. Surely that's what the state wants."

Brynn forced herself to breathe at a normal rate. Nothing would be served by coming off as an emotional basket case in front of Remi's social worker. Nick was right. She'd faced challenges she would have never expected and overcome them. She would make sure things worked out the right way with Remi.

"True." Jennifer smiled down at the baby. "And right now, the system is flooded with kids who need homes."

"Right before Christmas?" Brynn's heart broke for those children. "That's so unfair."

The social worker laughed without humor. "This job is a continual lesson in the unfairness of life. But Nick's right about this little sweetheart. She's doing great."

She'd held her breath when going over the details of the house fire, afraid it would be a strike against her. But the social worker had been surprisingly understanding about the entire situation.

Brynn straightened and took the baby from the woman. Remi immediately placed her head on

Brynn's shoulder and yawned. "Our sweetheart is tired and in need of a nap. If you don't need me for anything else, I'm going to take her upstairs."

Jennifer nodded. "Nick and I can finish up. Good luck with your house, Brynn. Call me when you're moved back in and we'll schedule a follow-up home visit. That will be the final step in the process of approving your foster application."

Brynn blinked, then nodded, taking care not to make eye contact with Nick. She'd almost forgotten this setup was temporary. Once she was approved, Nick wouldn't be a daily part of their lives anymore. It had only been a week since they'd been living under the same roof, but co-parenting with Nick felt as natural as slipping on a comfortable pair of shoes. Well, other than the part where she wanted to jump his hot body.

It would be a big adjustment to go back to the way things were before. One she didn't relish.

"I'll definitely call," she told the woman, then carried Remi up the stairs, still unwilling to meet Nick's gaze, although she felt him watching her.

She would deal with her emotions in private— wrestle them down to something less humiliating— before she faced him. Because if Nick looked in her eyes right now, he'd know. He'd know that she was ignoring the reality that Francesca might return. Brynn had pressed forward, making plans in her mind, carving out a future for herself and her two—definitely two—children. It was easier to ignore the past than admit how its shadow loomed across her life.

She'd scheduled herself to work from home today in order to meet with the social worker. Now she wondered if Jennifer assumed she was playing house with Nick, allowing herself to be caught up in a fantasy that would never materialize. Her face burned with embarrassment, like she'd been caught in class writing *Mrs. Nick Dunlap* in a notebook over and over. Like she'd once again reached above herself, wanting a man and a future she was never meant to have.

But she refused to believe Remi wasn't meant to be part of her family. The baby was already in her heart. Blinking away tears, she sang "Have Yourself a Merry Little Christmas" as she changed the girl's diaper and dimmed the lights in her room. The sweet, sad lyrics fit Brynn's mood, and Remi didn't seem to notice her melancholy.

The girl sighed as Brynn lay her on her back on the soft sheet, her eyes heavy with sleep. Brynn stood watching her for several minutes more. There was no way she wanted to go back downstairs if the social worker was still in the house.

In fact, she was half tempted to hide out in Nick's master bedroom until he left for work again. Give herself more time to regain her composure. It was amazing how much she'd made it through without falling apart, when now every tiny bump in the road seemed to send the apple cart of her emotions nearly tumbling to the ground.

She took a deep breath and let herself out of the room, closing the door behind her.

Nick stood across the hall in the doorway of his bedroom. He wore his dark uniform and looked like every fantasy she'd ever had come to life.

"I'm fine," she lied.

He held out a hand. "Come here."

Brynn felt like an emotional kamikaze as she moved forward, but right now she didn't have the strength to say no. The truth was she wanted the comfort. She wanted someone to tell her things would turn out all right because she desperately needed to believe it.

Christmas was in a couple of weeks. If ever there were a season for a miracle, Brynn could use one.

Nick drew her into the room, then wrapped her in his warm embrace. "I use the word *fine* when I mean the opposite," he said against the top of her head.

She breathed in the scent of him. "You never were great at grammar."

His laugh rumbled through her, loosening some of her anxiety.

"I feel so stupid," she admitted. "It isn't as if I don't know that Francesca could return and claim her baby. Honest to goodness, sometimes I log on to my email with my breath held and one eye squeezed shut. But every day, I believe more surely that Remi is supposed to be mine." She lifted her gaze to Nick's. "I'm broken, and it feels like that little girl is what's going to put me back together."

"You aren't broken," he said, smoothing a hand over her face. "You're totally together."

"That's what I want people to see." She bit down on her lower lip. "It's the role I play for Tyler. But inside I'm like a pile of smoldering ash. A shadow of who I want to be."

His brows drew together. "I don't believe it. Look at what you've done with your life since the summer. The job at the mill and going on dates."

"I bought new underwear," she said with a sniff.

"Right. Lots of changes."

"But something was missing…"

"Your old granny panties?"

Brynn choked out a laugh. "I never wore granny panties, just the regular five-pack of cotton bikinis."

He grinned, then blew out a strangled breath. "We need to stop talking about your undergarments. Tell me what was missing."

"Remi," Brynn answered simply. "As soon as I read Francesca's note, I knew that baby belonged with Tyler and me."

"There's no reason to believe she won't end up with you. No one has heard from Francesca. Based on how she seemed that first night at your house and her letter, she knows she isn't capable of raising a child."

Brynn nodded, wanting to believe him. "I know I'm borrowing trouble, but Remi already feels like mine. I don't know how to turn off my feelings for her, and yet if things don't turn out…"

"Then we'll get through it. Remember, you're not alone."

"I've always felt alone." She swallowed. "It still boggles my mind that I was married to a man for ten years and yet feel like I spent the past decade on my own."

"Brynn, I know I've said it before, but I'm sorry I pushed you toward Daniel back in high school. I have a stockpile of regrets in my life, but none as big as that one."

"It's not your regret to have." She could see the guilt in his gaze. She didn't want that. "I made the choice. No one forced me into it."

"There are so many things about that time I'd change. How I treated you." He sighed. "The way I acted with my family, especially Jack. If I hadn't been such a joker, maybe he wouldn't have felt like he had to be the perfect son to make up for it. Maybe he wouldn't have enlisted and then—"

"Hush." She hugged him closer. "You can't take responsibility for the choices your brother made any more than mine. We're quite a pair at the moment, both of us repenting for things we had no control over."

He turned his head into hers, and she felt more than heard his deep inhale, his face pressed against her skin. Then his lips touched the sensitive place behind her ear, and goose bumps erupted along her neck.

"Nick," she whispered, half moan and half plea.

"We're a pair," he repeated, his mouth moving along her jaw.

Then it was fused to hers and she lost herself in the feel of him, the barrage of sensations.

"I'm not going alone this time," she told him, as she broke the embrace. "Together or it stops now."

He raised a brow. "You'd say no to that kind of pleasure?"

"I want that." She exhaled a shaky breath. "Definitely. But I want it with you, Nick. I don't want you to worry about hurting me or to consider what's going to happen after Christmas. I want—need—to feel something."

"Me, too," he said softly and her heart, along with other parts of her body, leaped with joy.

Brynn's teenage crush on Nick seemed like a million years in the past. So much had happened to both of them, and right now she was grateful for the passing of time.

Because Brynn was no longer the infatuated schoolgirl who got tongue-tied and flustered at the drop of a hat. She was a woman, a mother, and she had enough experience in life to appreciate a moment like this without reservation.

They tugged on each other's clothes, the sensations swirling through her both familiar and new. She loved the feel of his skin against hers and the way he lowered her to the bed with the gentlest movement. He lavished attention on every part of her body until she trembled with need.

"I want you so badly," Nick whispered.

"I'm…right here," she said, even though what she meant was *I'm yours.* For as long as it lasted, she belonged to this man.

He looked deep into her eyes as he settled between her legs, and when he entered her, it was like coming home.

Brynn closed her eyes and let the pleasure of their joining carry her away. Nick covered her mouth with deep kisses. In truth, she was afraid to look at him, afraid of what she might reveal.

This was about now, and she wouldn't ruin it for either of them by second-guessing. Not that the force of their mutual desire could be derailed. Their bodies fell into a rhythm, and Brynn wondered if she'd been specifically made to be loved by this man.

It wasn't long before pressure began to build, driving her higher until she broke apart. Her body shattered with the pleasure of it and a sensation of completeness filled her as he found his own release. She held on to him, wanting nothing more than to savor this moment as long as possible.

He shifted to lie beside her, the quiet punctuated only by the sound of their breaths.

Brynn stretched out her toes and wiggled her fingers, surprised to find that her body looked the same as it had this morning. The last few minutes had changed everything about her. After a moment, Nick turned to her.

"Should we talk?" he asked, reluctance clear in his tone.

"Definitely not," she answered with a laugh, surprising both of them based on his sharp inhale.

She glanced over to find him staring at her with an inscrutable expression. "I mean it, Nick. My plate is spilling over with worries at the moment. I need something easy and fun. Something casual."

"And you and I are casual?"

"In this way." She nodded. "You like your women uncomplicated. I'm a tangled mess, but we can make this part of it straightforward."

He traced a fingertip along the ridge of her nose. "That's what you want?"

Her stomach clenched, but she nodded again. "It's what I need. What we both need."

"Okay, then," he agreed, although his tone had become strained. He was up and out of the bed an instant later. Her heart tripped in response to how easily he went along with her suggestion. As the door to the adjoining bathroom closed behind him, Brynn pulled off the covers and dressed.

Naked under a sheet was one thing, but now she needed the armor that clothes provided.

Nick didn't seem to share her modesty as he re-appeared in all his naked glory. Her knees shud-dered in response and she forced herself to look away. She walked to the mirror that hung above the dresser on the far wall and straightened both her hair and outfit.

Nothing good would come of anyone knowing that she and Nick had been together in this way.

"I need to get back to work," he said, and she could hear the frown in his voice.

"Sure. I've got a call scheduled in thirty minutes with Nanci and Mara to discuss a cupcake order for the next concert." She plastered on a bright smile. "If Remi doesn't take a long nap, I'll have time to run to the grocery before Tyler gets home from school."

Good lord. She wanted to slap herself. What kind of pathetically boring woman went from the best sex of her life to talking about groceries?

Nick was probably already regretting what they'd done, although he'd had a good enough time during the act based on his reaction.

"Not that you're under pressure to have dinner with us," she quickly added, unable to stem the tide of verbal diarrhea spewing from her mouth. "Having Remi, Tyler and me here must be disrupting your life." When he didn't respond, she continued, "Cramping your style."

From the reflection in the mirror, she could see he'd pulled on his boxers and uniform trousers, so Brynn felt it safe to turn around.

"What style?" he asked as he buttoned his dark navy department-issued shirt. His jaw was tight, his gaze hard.

"You know…" She laughed nervously. "Dates or whatever it is you do."

"Do you think I'm planning to go from sex with you to a date with another woman?" He made a noise that sounded suspiciously like a growl. "Like I'm trying to set some kind of land-speed record for being a heel."

"It's not like that," she protested. "*We're* not like that."

He tugged on his shirt cuffs and ran a hand through his hair, once again the tough law officer he'd matured into. "Are you still planning on finishing your twelve dates of Christmas?"

"The dates were a stupid joke from the start." She crossed her arms over her chest.

"Which doesn't answer the question."

"How would I have time to date between work, Tyler and adding Remi and the renovation in the mix? I barely managed it before all the changes to my life."

"Still not an answer."

"No." She rolled her eyes. "Not before this Christmas anyway. What man would want me given my current situation?"

"Any man in his right mind."

"Oh." Although he sounded angry—or at least frustrated—that was one of the nicest things someone had said to her. "Well, I'm putting the dating plan on hold. That doesn't mean you have to."

"Good to know," he ground out, then turned for the door before spinning back to face her. "Don't go to the grocery store."

Brynn inclined her head. She knew so much about Nick but could not begin to guess what he was thinking at this moment or why he seemed so irritated with her. Wasn't it every man's dream to have permission to date around? That's what ten years of marriage to a serial cheater had taught her.

"Why?"

"The holiday performance is tonight," he said. "I thought we could go out before heading over."

"You're going to the school?" She couldn't mask her surprise.

He tugged at the collar of his shirt like it was suddenly too tight. "Tyler invited me, so I planned on it. Unless that's a problem."

"I'm sure it would mean a lot to him to have you

there." She shrugged. "I figured I could take Remi and give you a night off from—" she waved her hands in the air like spastic birds "—all of this."

He closed his eyes for several seconds, and she could almost imagine him silently counting to ten. What was the problem?

"What time does he have to be at the school?" he asked instead of responding to her comment.

"Six."

He nodded. "I'll pick you up here at five, and we can get something at the downtown diner. Tyler mentioned he likes the fries."

"They're his favorite."

"Great." Nick's shoulders relaxed slightly. "If there's time, we could grab ice cream and drive around to look at lights after the performance."

Brynn felt her mouth drop open and snapped it shut. "Sure. That would be great."

"Great," he repeated.

"Does *great* mean the opposite in the way *fine* does?" she asked, referring to his earlier comment.

He shook his head and his mouth lifted into a half smile. "It means we're going to have a great time tonight."

"Okay," she agreed, wondering why she was suddenly breathless again. "We'll see you at five."

His grin widened. Had they just made progress on some problem she wasn't even aware of? "It's a date," he said softly, then disappeared into the hall.

A date?

Alone in the room, Brynn sank down to the edge of the bed. *Could this day get any stranger?* she thought, as she smoothed a hand over the comforter. The best sex of her life and now a date—a date—with Nick Dunlap. Talk about checking off the list of Christmas miracles.

Chapter Thirteen

Nick walked toward his front door just before five o'clock, nerves dancing through his stomach. His friends would get a laugh out of that, and he couldn't blame them.

Who got nervous approaching the house they'd lived in for the past five years?

Night was descending over the town, and already Christmas lights glowed from the homes around him. Starlight might not get much snow or below-freezing temperatures, but its residents still went all out for the holiday like they were living at the North Pole.

"I'm hungry for fries." Tyler opened the door as

Nick got to the top step. The boy zipped out past him before Nick had a chance to respond.

"You're not wearing your uniform."

He glanced up to find Brynn standing in the doorway. Remi's infant seat was on the floor next to her.

"I keep a change of clothes at the office," he explained, suddenly self-conscious and not sure why. Instead of his uniform, he'd put on a pair of khaki pants and a button-down shirt. Nothing special, but Brynn stared at him like he'd shown up in a tux and tails. "It's easier that way."

She licked her lips, and awareness zinged across his skin in response.

"These are for you." He shoved the bouquet of daisies he'd bought from the local florist toward her.

Her brows puckered. "Why?"

Nick scratched his jaw. "I thought you'd like them. I remember that yellow was your favorite. Or used to be. I guess I don't know—"

"It's still my favorite." She took the flowers from him, almost reluctantly, and lifted them to her nose. "Thank you. They're beautiful."

"Come on," Tyler called from the driveway. "I'm starving."

"I'll get Remi and Ty settled if you want to put them in water."

"Okay," she whispered, still staring at the flowers.

"Is something wrong?" he asked. "Did I mess up again?"

"Not at all." She flashed a watery smile. "Pay no attention to me."

"I don't think that's possible. Brynn, what's going on?"

"The flowers are beautiful," she repeated with a small shake of her head. "I love them."

She turned for the kitchen. Still puzzled at her response, he picked up the car seat and headed for his truck. Tyler climbed into the back seat, talking about the perfect ketchup-to-fry ratio as Nick clipped Remi into the seat's base.

He wasn't sure what the hell had happened on his porch, but he decided the best course of action was to press forward. Nick had done a lot of thinking during his shift today, about Brynn giving up on dating—which he was all for—and what Parker and Finn had told him about her friends wanting to find a man for her.

He'd made a vow to himself the night of the tree lighting that he would give Brynn the Christmas she deserved. If that included finishing the ridiculous commitment to twelve dates, he'd give her those dates.

Even if he couldn't give her more. Even if he refused to admit to himself he wanted more.

He adjusted the radio to a station playing holiday classics as she got into the truck a few minutes later.

"All set?" he asked, glancing at her and relieved to see she looked less astonished and more like her normal, controlled self.

She nodded. "I'm excited for the winter concert." She looked over her shoulder toward Tyler in the back seat. "You're going to be the best narrator Starlight has ever seen."

Each year, the elementary school children performed skits and songs around the theme of winter and peace on earth. Nick knew Brynn was grateful Tyler seemed happy about his expanded role in the production and that he wasn't focusing on the fact that his father wasn't there to see him perform.

"Remember last year I had to be one of the sheeps," Tyler answered. "That's what the little kids have to be, but now I'm a big kid so I get actual lines. Someday Remi will be a sheep."

"She's got a few years before that happens," Brynn answered with a tight laugh.

He had a feeling she was thinking about the potential of Francesca returning. He wished he could take the worry from her mind, but even he couldn't predict the future.

"Remind me to show you the scar I've got on the back of my head," he said, meeting Tyler's gaze in the rearview mirror. "When your mom and I were in third grade, we had to do this holiday concert, and it was so hot in the gymnasium that I passed out. Fell right off the bleachers and knocked my head on one corner. I ended up with twelve stitches."

"Seriously?" Ty sounded awestruck.

"Not only did Nick pass out," Brynn added, "but two other girls in the class followed suit when they saw the blood. It was a gruesome ending to the concert."

The boy laughed. "That sounds awesome."

"Other than Nick getting hurt," Brynn said, her tone gently chiding. "It was scary."

"I milked the attention for all I could," Nick told the boy. "Your mom brought over chocolate chip cookies to make me feel better."

"She makes the best cookies," Tyler confirmed, then began to sing along with Bing Crosby as a popular holiday tune filled the cab's interior.

Brynn joined her son, and Nick thought about all the times the woman next to him had been a good friend to him. She'd been his biggest cheerleader for sports, tutored him in every core subject and been the one person in his life to make him believe he didn't come up short in comparison to his brother. In return, he'd alternately taken her for granted and ignored her outright.

Nick knew he had to stop dwelling on what an idiot he'd been in the past. It would do no good and the best he could hope for was to change going forward.

He pulled into the parking lot of the popular local

restaurant, unsurprised to see that it was already nearly filled.

"Oh, no." Brynn sucked in a breath. "It looks like there's a wait. We might not have time—"

"I called ahead," Nick told her with a smile.

She frowned. "Stan doesn't take reservations."

"Your friendly neighborhood police chief might have helped his son out of a bind a few years back." Nick winked. "I've got connections."

"Lucky you," she murmured, grinning at him.

Lucky indeed, Nick thought, as they walked toward the entrance. He placed a hand on the small of Brynn's back as Stan showed them to a table near the front of the restaurant. He couldn't help his need to claim her, at least temporarily.

Nick had always thought he was fine on his own, the stereotypical "lone wolf" lawman. He'd figured it was his destiny. But the more time he spent with Brynn, the more he wanted something different. The more he believed he might be able to claim a future he'd never expected.

"People are staring," she said under her breath, as she shrugged out of her wool coat.

"It's because you look so pretty tonight." Affection bloomed in his chest as color stained her cheeks.

"I doubt that." She pulled a plastic spinning wheel with a suction on the bottom out of the diaper bag and stuck it to the table in front of Remi's high chair. "The town gossips are going to have a field day seeing us like this."

"Like what?" He shrugged. "We've been friends most of our lives, and now we have Remi as a connection between us."

"For now," she said.

He nodded, although he didn't want to consider the temporary nature of their arrangement. "I'm not worried about what other people think." He ruffled Tyler's thick mop of hair. "I'm too busy plotting how I'm going to steal this guy's fries."

"No way," the boy said, then his eyes went wide as a waitress put down a big plate of the restaurant's famous french fries in the middle of the table.

"Stan sent these over for you to enjoy before your food comes." The waitress was in her midfifties with her hair pulled back into a low ponytail. "Are you ready to order or do you need a few minutes?"

"Ready," Tyler answered and rattled off his order, adding a *please* at the end, then grinning at his mother.

Brynn and Nick ordered as well, and Remi smiled at the waitress.

"Your daughter is adorable," the woman said to Brynn. "She's a perfect mix between you and your husband."

Nick felt a combination of happiness and unease rush through him. It made sense that a stranger would assume he was the baby's father. They were out for what looked like a perfectly normal family dinner. But he didn't want the presumption to add to Brynn's anxiety.

He kept his features neutral as he glanced toward Brynn. Her smile looked forced but didn't waver. "She's a sweet girl."

Remi babbled excitedly as if to verify that assessment.

"She sure is. I'll get those orders right in," the waitress said.

"Will you pass me the crayons?" Tyler asked, seemingly unaware of the awkward tension that had descended over their group. He gestured to the plastic cup in the center of the table.

Nick reached for it, his fingers grazing Brynn's as she did the same. She immediately drew back as if his touch was electric. Nick handed the cup to the boy, who began to complete a word search printed on the paper kids' menu.

"It's crowded for a weeknight," Brynn said, as she glanced around the restaurant.

He nodded. "There aren't a lot of options for casual dinners in Starlight."

She blew out a shaky laugh, then visibly relaxed her shoulders. "What the waitress said wasn't a big deal."

Nick couldn't decide which one of them she was trying to convince.

"It's an obvious assumption if you don't know us."

It was his turn to laugh. "I'm not used to someone in town not being able to identify me. I kind of liked it."

Her eyes widened a fraction, and he wondered if she thought he was referring to being unrecognized or someone mistaking him for her husband. Honestly, it was a little of both, but he had no intention of admitting that.

"It's good to have new people come to town." She drew one finger around the rim of her water glass. "Josh and I are working on plans for an addition to the mill that would include a sit-down restaurant. I think it would attract more locals as well as out-of-town visitors."

"That's a great idea," he told her. "Although some of the food-truck owners might be disappointed. I heard you have a waiting list for trucks on-site during weekends."

Her grin was natural now. "We still want to utilize the trucks. The response to our theme nights has been overwhelming."

"You're doing a great job with the marketing. Everyone says so."

"I don't know about everyone." She rolled her eyes. "There are a number of old-timers around who aren't thrilled about the town's new growth. But even they can't deny the refreshed energy of the community. It feels good to be a part of it, and

I'm so grateful to Josh and Parker for giving me a chance."

They continued to talk about her work and his job. Nick appreciated that the tension from earlier had disappeared, even when the waitress brought their food and Stan stopped by the table. The older man commented on how pretty Brynn and Remi looked, but Brynn only blushed and thanked him for the compliment.

By the time they got to the school, Nick felt calmer than he had in days. Maybe they could forge ahead with a fresh start, after all.

Brynn looked at her reflection in the hazy mirror above the girls' bathroom sink down the hall from the school's auditorium. Nick had dropped her off with Tyler so she could walk him to his classroom, where the students were meeting before the start of the performance.

She'd gotten waylaid talking to the teacher she'd subbed for the previous semester, when the young mom had been on maternity leave, and then made a quick stop at the bathroom because she needed a quiet minute to herself. Nick texted that he'd gotten seats near the aisle in case Remi needed to be whisked out midperformance.

Brynn didn't want to compare tonight to the years she and Daniel had attended the school performances together. He'd never been all that interested in young kids doing their thing on stage, and she'd had to cajole and threaten him into coming with her every year, making sure she showed enough enthusiasm before and after the performance that Tyler wouldn't notice his father's lack of interest.

Nick acted like he was going to a Broadway play, and his excitement—even if it was all for Ty's benefit—melted her heart. As if she needed another reason to fall for Nick Dunlap.

The door to the restroom opened, and she turned as Cassie Monaghan entered. Cassie had been in the same graduating class as Brynn, although they hadn't run in anywhere near the same circles. Brynn had stuck with the misfits other than when she was trailing around after Nick and his buddies like some kind of worshipful sidekick.

Cassie, on the other hand, had been one of the "it" girls. She and her friends had run the school, from the cheer team to homecoming and prom courts. In fact, Cassie had been Nick's date to senior prom. The memory burned like acid in Brynn's gut even now. There were plenty of good things about living in a small town, but she didn't consider unwanted reminders of the past part of that.

"Hey, Cass." Brynn smiled as she tugged a paper towel from the dispenser. "I didn't know you were back in town."

"Just until after Christmas." The other woman

smirked. "I got hired at a new salon in Portland, so I took a week off to recharge."

"That's great." Somewhere in the back of her mind, Brynn knew Cassie was a hairdresser. She certainly had a beautiful mane of thick, perfectly curled blond hair. In fact, the woman was perfectly turned out from the top of her shiny hair to her shapely legs tucked into red cowboy boots. She looked as polished and intimidating as she had a decade earlier.

Brynn shifted when Cassie continued to block her way to the door and resisted the urge to scratch at her lace bra, which suddenly felt itchy in all the wrong places. She glanced down at the simple black shift she wore with colorful patterned clogs. She might not work at the elementary school any longer, but she still dressed the part. Maybe it was time for an update of more than just her undergarments.

"It's nice of you to come to the performance. I'm sure Gillian is glad to have you here. She'll do great." Cassie's niece, Gillian, one of Tyler's classmates, was the star of the show this year.

When Cassie didn't respond, Brynn made to move past her. The other woman grabbed her arm. "He's not going to fall for you," she said, her voice barely above a whisper. "You weren't his type in high school, and you aren't now."

Brynn's stomach dipped. "I don't know what

you're talking about." She managed to keep her voice steady.

"Nick," Cassie clarified, although she must know Brynn wasn't that dense. "We've stayed in contact over the years, you know."

"Yeah," Brynn answered, even though she'd known nothing of the sort. But Starlight was a small town with one popular bar for locals and tourists alike. She'd seen Cassie around during holidays and breaks, so it shouldn't surprise her that Nick had, as well. Heck, Daniel had even mentioned running into her at Trophy Room a few times over the years. The sick pit in Brynn's stomach gaped wider. For all she knew, her husband had cheated on her with this woman.

"We get together when I come back." She leaned in closer. "You know what I mean by together, right?"

Brynn didn't bother to answer.

"This week I text him and he tells me he's too busy for a drink."

"Maybe he's too busy," Brynn said through clenched teeth. "Or maybe you should take a hint."

"Nick and I are cut from the same cloth." Cassie's fingers dug into Brynn's skin, and she yanked away from the painful grasp. "We like our relationships straightforward, no-strings-attached. You're the biggest ball of tangled yarn I've ever seen, Brynn Hale. Between getting yourself knocked up, a husband who couldn't keep it in his pants and now taking on one of his bastards, you're a bigger mess now than you ever were. You should have stayed the mousy wallflower. Nick will never let himself be saddled with you and your two sad-sack children and if you think—"

Brynn's arm shot out and before she knew what she was doing, Cassie's back was up against the cold tile wall of the bathroom with Brynn's forearm pinning her so she couldn't move. Rage bubbled up inside Brynn, hot and fiery, in a way she barely recognized. It coursed through her like molten lava, giving her a ferocity she hadn't known she possessed.

She'd taken a lot of grief, pity and judgment over the years. She could deal with it, but there was no way she would let anyone disparage either of her children.

And they were both hers. No matter what the future held for Remi, Brynn knew without a shadow of a doubt that she would always love that girl with her entire heart.

"You don't know Nick, and you never have." She leaned in, satisfied when Cassie's heavily mascaraed eyes widened in shock. "And you definitely don't know me or my children. Let me tell you that I'm proud of the life I've made for myself and them."

"That baby isn't even yours," the other woman said on a hiss of breath.

"She needs a mother, and I'm honored to fill that

role. I don't care what you or anyone else thinks about it." She released Cassie and stepped back. "Your opinion means nothing to me. I have a feeling you mean less than nothing to Nick." She smiled broadly. "Merry Christmas, Cassie," she said and walked out of the bathroom.

She walked to the auditorium with her head held high, greeting the people she passed in the hall by name or smiling at the ones she didn't recognize. The rows of chairs were half-full, and she quickly found Nick and took a seat next to him.

"What's wrong?" he asked immediately, concern filling his gaze. He held Remi on his lap, and to Brynn's great joy, the baby reached for her.

"Everything's fine," she said, lifting the girl into her arms. "I ran into Cassie Monaghan in the bathroom."

Nick muttered a curse.

Brynn kept the smile on her face as she snuggled the baby to her chest. To anyone watching her—and she could feel the weight of multiple stares—there was no outward sign of the turmoil racing through her body.

"If you want to go out with her, or hook up, or whatever it is you two do over the holidays, don't let me or Remi stop you."

She heard his sharp intake of breath.

"I haven't gone out with Cassie in years," he said, voice tight. "I have no plan to start now."

"Anyone," Brynn modified. "If you want to go out with anyone, it's—"

"No." He placed a heavy hand on her leg, and she wished she could stop her reaction to his touch, but it felt too good. Too right. "How many times do I have to say it before you'll believe me, Brynn? I don't want anyone else. I'm happy with you. I know that it's not permanent, that you don't think of me in that way. I'm not going to push you away. But I've missed you. If nothing else, believe that."

She gave a shaky nod, grateful when the elementary school's principal took the stage to begin the show. Her mind spun at the sincerity in Nick's tone. Was he trying to placate her, or had he spoken the truth? How could he think she wouldn't see him as someone who could be a permanent part of her life?

Was it possible that he doubted her commitment to him as much as she doubted his? In her wildest fantasies, she'd never considered a world where Nick Dunlap could be hurt by her. Brynn didn't hurt people. She was on the receiving end of emotional suffering and had gotten used to laughing it off. Anything else was like the world tilting in a way she couldn't understand.

She might not be able to comprehend this new revelation, but her heart stammered at the simple idea that Nick could want her in the same way she wanted him. He squeezed her leg, and she flashed a quick smile in return, careful not to make eye contact with him. The lights went down in the auditorium and she focused on the students filing out onto the stage. Once again, Nick had changed everything for her.

Chapter Fourteen

Nick sat on the edge of the mattress later that night, elbows on his knees and head in his hands. His mind raced in a million different directions, but at the end, all of them led back to the same place.

Brynn.

He'd thought he left his stupid ego moves behind years ago but realized now that he was still an idiot. His big plan to give her some sort of magical Christmas and the dates she seemed to want had blown up in his face. Not that she realized it. No one would because Nick was too good at keeping his feelings hidden.

Well, his friends had an inkling, but that stemmed

more from the way he'd decided he felt about her too late in high school than anything now. Back then, she'd been the one that got away. The one he'd pushed away.

He'd assumed his inability to get over Brynn had more to do with a mix of his competitive nature and the fact that he'd gotten used to her constant presence than true heartbreak. It didn't matter that his chest had ached every time he saw her in town, either with Daniel and Tyler or on her own. He'd taken to avoiding her over the years because that helped dull the pain. Pain he attributed to guilt.

Daniel Hale had been a horrible husband, and Nick knew Brynn would have never ended up with the man if Nick hadn't arranged that fateful prom date.

Despite everything, he'd always assumed he was in control. But it didn't matter how high he built his defenses. They were nothing Brynn couldn't scale. Hell, she didn't even have to work at it. In truth, she held the key to his heart and always had.

Where did that leave him?

He looked up at the knock on the door and his heart stammered against his ribs as the woman who consumed his thoughts beyond all reason stepped into his office.

"I wanted to thank you again for tonight," she said, her tone soft, hesitant. Her hair was down, tucked back behind her ears, and she wore the thickest, fuzziest robe he'd ever seen. The robe was so big and bulky it almost swallowed her whole. Even with the shapeless fabric engulfing her, his body immediately sprang to life. Her scent floated to him, and his fingers itched to pull her close. He tucked his hands under his thighs and nodded.

"It was fun," he said, laughing at the unbelieving lift of her brow. "I mean it. I haven't been to a school event since we were that age. Watching the kids do their thing reminded me of the real meaning of the holidays. People get so worked up about presents and the commercial stuff, but it's most important to make time for those kinds of moments."

"Tell that to all the parents scrambling to finish Christmas shopping."

"Yeah." He shrugged. "I guess I don't understand what it's like."

"You understand plenty," she said and took a step forward. "You've made this past week bearable. I'm not sure Tyler will want to go home when the renovations are complete. He's having too much fun with you."

"It's Remi. He likes being around her." Nick ignored the ping in his heart at the thought he might be important to the boy. "Once she's with you, he won't even think about me."

"I'll think about you," she said, her voice low. She gave a strangled laugh. "I think about you far too much for my own good."

"Brynn." He wanted to give her some reassurance, to explain he was the one in danger of losing his heart and maybe his mind. That she held more sway over him than he ever could have imagined. But the words caught in his throat when she locked the door to his office and then untied the belt of her robe.

The fuzzy material opened, revealing a red slip made of silk and lace. He made a sound—nothing coherent—a guttural noise somewhere between a groan and a growl.

"I bought this a while ago," she said when she stood directly in front of him. "After…this summer… I made a whole list of things I wanted to do and try."

"And killing me was at the top?" he managed to choke out.

She grinned, and the knowing and utterly feminine smile did wicked things to his body.

"I don't want to kill you," she assured him, as she shifted so that the robe fell to the floor at her feet.

The air whooshed out of Nick's lungs.

"But I wanted to make sure you'd notice."

He laughed. "I thought you were the sexiest thing I'd ever seen wearing a fuzzy robe. I'm not sure I'm equipped to handle you like this."

"And yet you'll try?" She raised a brow. "Because if I went to the trouble for nothing, it's going to make me so sad."

The small smile that played around the corners

of her mouth belied her words. She looked anything but sad. She was beautiful and radiant and absolutely irresistible. He reached for her and tugged her between his legs. His hands splayed across the silky fabric that covered her hips.

"For as long as you'll let me," he promised.

She bent her head and their mouths fused together as his hands slid over the satiny fabric. He pulled the slip over her head, then covered the tight peak of her breast with his mouth, and the soft needy sound she made almost undid him. He pulled her with him onto the mattress, and they were a tangle of limbs—kissing and touching until he lost track of where he ended and she began.

When he couldn't wait any longer, Nick grabbed a condom wrapper and sheathed himself, then entered her in one long slow stroke. It felt different than before. Brynn didn't hold anything back, and the way she allowed herself to be exposed—both physically and emotionally—rocked him to his core. He couldn't imagine a time in his life when he wouldn't want this. Wouldn't want her.

He tried to hold back even as his desire surged forward. Physical need and emotion didn't meld for him. They'd always been separate, easy for him to keep different parts of his life in segregated boxes. But the way he felt with Brynn knocked away everything he'd known before. His control. His boundaries. There was nothing between them. She knew him better than anyone ever had, and she chose him anyway.

And he knew her—wanted to know her more. To understand every nook and cranny of her soul. Something both sharp and sweet blossomed in his chest as the physical pressure built, so much more than he expected when she shuddered and cried out beneath him. It was all he needed to push him over the edge of release. How was it possible he'd gone all these years without this kind of soul-baring intimacy?

Maybe because it made him vulnerable. He was like a lovesick puppy, ready to turn over and expose all his soft bits to this woman. Nick would rather go out on a million life-threatening calls at the station than set himself up for the kind of potential pain he risked if things didn't work out. And it wasn't only his heart. Now that Brynn was back in his life, he realized how he'd missed her friendship. He'd missed talking to her and hearing her take on every slight detail of their lives.

He didn't want to lose any of it.

That line of thinking got him nowhere, especially when he'd just had the best damn sex of his life. What was wrong with him, to go looking for trouble before it even showed up on his doorstep?

He lifted his head and her eyes fluttered open, half-dazed but filled with the affection he craved.

"Hi," she whispered.

"Hi, yourself." He dropped a kiss on the tip of her nose.

She smiled at him, almost shyly. "I'm going to say my lingerie worked."

"The slip was sexy as hell, but you're all I need. Silk or a fuzzy bathrobe. Either works for me, Brynn. As long as it's you."

"You make me feel good," she told him.

"That's my pl—"

"Hey." Panic gripped him when a tear slid from the corner of her eye. "What's wrong?"

She shook her head and laughed. "I didn't expect… This wasn't what… I'm happy."

Those two words made him feel ten feet tall. "Me, too," he told her, then excused himself to the bathroom. He climbed back into the bed with her, pulling her close. Her leg wrapped around his hip and her delicate fingers curled over his chest.

"I'm happy you're happy," he said, breathing in her sweetness.

They were silent for several moments and then she said quietly, "I don't trust happiness."

"Oh, honey." He squeezed her shoulder. "Do you trust me?"

He didn't like how long it took her to answer. "I want to."

"I'm going to give you every reason to trust me. To believe your happiness is my top priority."

"You have," she said, propping herself on an

elbow. "You've been amazing, Nick. I don't know how I'll ever repay you for your generosity."

He frowned. Something about her words made it sound like she'd need to repay him because he was doing her a favor. That once this ended she could bake a cake or bring over dinner and a bottle of wine as a thank-you and they'd be done.

Nick didn't like that thought, but he was still afraid to push her. Afraid to reveal he might need her more than she needed him.

"I care about you, Brynn." He smoothed a lock of dark hair away from her face. "About Tyler and Remi, too. No repayment needed."

She smiled again and then yawned. "I should go back upstairs. Tyler is a sound sleeper now, but I'd hate for him to wake up and not find me across the hall."

It was difficult to let her go, but Nick forced himself to release her. "Close your eyes," she told him, as she scooted to the far edge of the foam mattress.

His brows furrowed and amusement spiked in his chest. "I've seen you naked," he reminded her. "In fact, I've kissed about every inch of your body."

"It's different." She leveled him with a steely stare. "Eyes closed. I mean it, Nick."

"Fine," he answered with an amused sigh.

"No peeking," she commanded, and he felt the lift of the mattress when she got up. It only took a few seconds before she gave him the go ahead to open his eyes again.

Once again, she was bundled up in the fluffy robe. A strip of red lace peeked out from the pocket, sending his body into overdrive once again at the memory of his hands and mouth all over her body.

"Good night, Nick," she said, bending to kiss his cheek. "Thank you for a lovely evening."

He almost laughed at the simple statement. Leave it to Brynn to be unfailingly polite after raking her fingernails across his back minutes earlier.

When he was alone again, he closed his eyes and drifted off to sleep with every hope he'd find a way to dream about the woman sleeping upstairs.

"She's adorable."

Brynn watched as Ella Samuelson, Finn's younger sister, lifted Remi into her arms. The woman, who was a year or so younger than Brynn, looked comfortable with the baby, which Brynn appreciated.

"That's the consensus." Brynn smiled. She continued wrapping presents as they spoke. "I appreciate you agreeing to start right away. I'm sure you have a lot of catching up to do with your family now that you're back."

Ella shrugged and kept her attention focused on Remi. "I need a little distraction in my life right now." She had the same blue eyes as her brother, but her hair was several shades lighter and she had the kind of loose-limbed grace Brynn could only dream about possessing. "Starlight has changed since I left, but my feelings about the town haven't caught up. Coming home felt like the right decision when I was sitting in a hut in a Brazilian rain forest. The reality of being here is almost as foreign as any of the places I've traveled to in the past few years."

"It must have been exciting to see so much of the world." Brynn sighed. She'd been as far as Chicago for a high school choir trip but hadn't traveled out of the country once in her life. When her friends had been off to college and life adventures, she'd been busy raising Tyler.

"I loved getting to experience different cultures and meet people from all kinds of backgrounds." Ella bit down on her lower lip. "After a while, living out of a duffel bag gets old, even with a spectacular view."

"Can I ask you a personal question?" Brynn paused with a roll of tape in her hand and studied the other woman.

"Sure," Ella agreed readily despite the hesitation in her tone. "I appreciate that we skipped over the formal interview for the nanny position but I expected you to have questions about me and my qualifications."

"You're a pediatric nurse," Brynn said with a laugh. "You're overqualified to be a nanny. Which leads to my question. Why?" She shook her head.

"I'm sure you could get hired immediately at the local hospital. Why do you want to be a nanny with your impressive résumé?"

Ella handed Remi a plastic giraffe. The girl kicked her feet and shoved the toy into her mouth to investigate. "Because I don't want to be impressive right now," Ella answered. "I want to be happy." She met Brynn's gaze and her gaze softened. "I haven't stayed in the same place for more than six months in the past five years. I'm not expecting my return to Starlight to be permanent. I need a break, but I also want to stay busy. Taking care of this little cutie will allow me to do both."

"Something happened to you," Brynn said quietly.

Ella's smile was forced. "Lots of things happened to me. I'm not special, and my story isn't unique. Maybe it's burnout at twenty-seven, which sounds pathetic. Still, I need a break."

"I appreciate you taking that break with Remi. Finn and Kaitlin are so glad you're here," Brynn told her.

"I never expected to see my brother settled down and ready to get married. He really loves her."

"She's an amazing person. Kaitlin is devoted to both Finn and your father. She's helped them get close again."

Ella made a face. "I'm still having trouble wrapping my mind around the fact that my dad and my brother are close." She blew out a sharp laugh. "This is going to sound awful, but it feels like Finn is being disloyal. The one thing that bonded us was always mutual disdain for our father. Now I'm the one on the outside, and they're all chummy. I can't get over it."

"You're not on the outside," Brynn said, hearing the pain in the other woman's voice. "It means a lot to both of them that you're here."

"I'm not staying," Ella said suddenly. "Two months at the most and then I might travel a bit on my own before the new contract with Traveling Nurses starts again. I took a six-month leave."

"It's amazing that you have so many options."

"It's kind of amazing that you have so many presents to wrap," Ella replied with a laugh.

"I want this to be Tyler's best Christmas ever." Brynn wrapped a swath of colorful paper around a microscope box. "I know I went overboard. I'm like most people around the holidays. I can talk a good game about the point of the season not being materialistic, but I get sucked right down the consumer rabbit hole." She eyed the pile of gifts she'd stacked on the far end of the table. "Are you disgusted by my rampant consumerism? It probably looks like gluttony to you."

"It looks like you're overcompensating for sure."

Brynn winced at Ella's honesty. "Well, you aren't wrong."

Ella grinned at Remi. "I remember when you got pregnant," she said suddenly. "I was a junior, and it was all anyone could talk about."

"A cautionary tale," Brynn murmured with a dry laugh. "I'm sure my story was used as an example of the importance of abstinence for parents around here for years. The best birth control money couldn't buy."

"I never thought about it that way," Ella said softly. "I thought it was amazing you kept your head held high and did what needed to get done. Back in high school, I liked to rebel for the sake of rebelling. But it was stupid. You made decisions about what was going to happen with your life, and you didn't care what anyone else thought. You were a true maverick."

"I cared," Brynn whispered. "I just cared about my son more."

"Like you care about Remi."

"My mother is certain I'm trying to ruin her life."

Ella sucked in a breath. "By adopting a baby?"

"She doesn't think I can handle another child, and she definitely objects to the circumstances of Remi's birth."

"You don't have your mother's support?" Ella sounded genuinely shocked.

Brynn shook her head, trying to ignore the ache in her chest. "She's also angry that Nick is involved and that his mom has been helping with her. We were neighbors growing up, and my mom always felt like his mom judged her for being a single parent. She hated that and didn't want it for me. When I got pregnant, she made sure I knew getting Daniel to marry me was the highest priority." She rolled her eyes. "That didn't work out the way she expected and, of course, it had to be my fault. She's never really gotten over her anger at how my life turned out, and Remi adds to it. It makes me a topic for gossips in town, and my mother hates feeling like she's associated with gossip."

"Those people are jerks," Ella said. "And stupid. Stupid jerks."

"I've gotten used to people not expecting much of me," Brynn said with a quiet laugh.

"No one should get used to that," Ella countered.

"Maybe, but it's what I know."

"How did Nick get involved in this?" Ella asked, glancing around the living room. "I had such a little-sister crush on both him and Parker when I was in high school. He was hot as a five-alarm fire but kind of a selfish prick, you know?"

Brynn grinned. "Trust me, I know. And I know all about crushing on him. He's grown up a lot since then. I need to be approved as a foster parent, so he agreed to take in Remi so I could be close to her."

"You two were besties back in the day, right?"

"Something like that."

"He seems different now." Ella tapped a finger

against her chin. "Not just grown up like Finn and Parker. He's more serious. He used to crack jokes and prank people all the time. Now he's almost subdued."

"His brother died in combat while Nick was away at college," Brynn explained. "His dad had a fatal heart attack shortly after. Coming back to Starlight to help his mom changed him."

"I get that," Ella murmured.

"You were a teenager when your mom died." Brynn turned fully to face the other woman. Ella's rosy complexion had gone pale as if the memory still caused her physical pain. "That's a hard age to lose a parent."

Ella flashed a tight smile. "Especially when the one who's left doesn't like you very much."

"Are things still rough with your dad? Is that why you've come home? I heard he's starting another round of cancer treatment."

Remi let out a small cry, and Ella picked her up, then began to sway back and forth as she rubbed the baby's back. She kept her head down for several long seconds, and when she finally looked up, Brynn saw tears swimming in her eyes.

"Oh, I'm sorry." Brynn immediately stood and reached for the baby. "I didn't mean to upset you. We've been talking so freely. I've told you more about my emotional scars in one conversation than most of my friends know. If I crossed a line..."

"You didn't." Ella swiped at her cheeks. "It's so strange, this business of bursting into tears at the drop of a hat. I spent years working with struggling populations. I've held children when they've taken their last breath and comforted mothers who've lost their babies to disease and illness. I managed all of it with a professionalism that sometimes worried the people I worked with. Apparently, I was compartmentalizing my feelings. As of six months ago, all of the compartments were full. Everything that happens affects me until I feel like I'm being crushed under the emotional weight of it."

"Oh, Ella. I can only imagine how tough that is."

Ella sniffed. "I wish I could say I came back to patch things up with my dad. It would be the noble thing to do. I bet it would be how you'd handle it. Mainly, I ran away from my life with my tail between my legs. Starlight was the only place I could think of going where I might distract myself from everything I can't stop feeling. But I've been here three days and I've barely spoken to my dad. I'm staying in his guesthouse and I'm still so damn angry at how he treated Finn and me after my mom died that I don't know what to say."

"That's understandable," Brynn said, even though she didn't understand it. She couldn't imagine having that sort of anger at anyone. Maybe it's why she'd been such a pushover in her marriage.

"I'm angry with Finn, too," Ella admitted on a

rush of air. "The biggest bond we had was our animosity toward Dad. Now I'm this lonely, angry woman who can't seem to stop crying." She gave a watery laugh. "I bet you wish you'd known all this before you hired me to take care of Remi."

"It wouldn't have changed anything," Brynn told her.

"You're too nice of a person."

"I get that a lot."

"I'm not nearly nice enough."

Brynn kissed Remi's cheek when the little girl snuggled against her. "You have a big heart, Ella. I can tell. It might feel a bit bruised right now, but hearts can heal. Trust me. I'm an expert."

"This may be none of my business, but are you and Nick an item?"

Brynn wasn't sure how to explain what was between her and Nick, but the word *item* didn't begin to do her emotions justice.

"*Complicated* is the best way to describe it," she said with a laugh. Remi fussed and wiggled in her arms. She checked her watch. "Time for a diaper change and a nap," she told the girl with another soft kiss to the head.

"I'll take her up," Ella offered. "It will be good to see if she'll go down for me without a fuss."

Brynn gave Remi to the other woman reluctantly. It was difficult to let the baby go, but she knew Remi was in good hands with Finn's sister.

She checked the messages on her phone after Ella headed upstairs. Josh had texted to tell her they were still planning to finish the work as promised, so she could prepare to return to her house on Christmas Eve.

A flood of conflicting emotions washed through her. On one hand, she was grateful Josh's crew had stayed on schedule, a rarity in the world of construction. On the other, she felt a pang of sadness about not being with Nick on Christmas morning. Over the past few days, his house had come to feel like home.

She'd talked to Jennifer at social services, and as soon as the background check came back, Brynn would be approved as Remi's foster parent.

And Nick would be free of her.

A thought that pained her more than anything else.

Chapter Fifteen

"I mean it, Marianne. Go take care of your yule log."

The station's longtime receptionist chuckled as she straightened from her desk and began to load her tote bag. "That sounds kind of dirty, Chief," she told him with a wink. "I'm going to have to tell Daryll you were talking about my yule log."

Nick rolled his eyes even as he felt a blush rise to his cheeks. Marianne had a bawdy sense of humor for a woman pushing seventy and took great pleasure in embarrassing Nick and his deputies. She'd been a fixture at the department since way before Nick's time, and normally was the calmest, most easygoing woman on the planet.

But it was three days before Christmas, and something had gone wrong with the recipe she'd made for a family dinner tonight.

"In all seriousness," she said, patting his hand. "I appreciate it. Daryll hasn't been doing too well, and it means a lot that all our kids are coming back to celebrate Christmas with us a couple days early. It's different when they have kids of their own, so I don't take it for granted," she sniffed. "That dessert has been my tradition since they were toddlers baking in the kitchen with me. It has to be right."

"Then go make it right," he told her. The station was quiet, with only a few of his staff out on calls.

Just as he turned to head back to his office, the door opened and Jennifer Ryan walked in. Nick's stomach dropped as the social worker gave him a wan smile.

"Did we have an appointment?" he asked, an uncomfortable shiver passing through him.

"No. Can we talk in your office?"

Her tone did nothing to ease his growing panic, but he didn't want to alert Marianne or any of the deputies still in the station that something might be wrong.

"Remi's mother contacted the department this morning," Jennifer said as soon as the door clicked shut.

Nick's hand squeezed the knob as he forced his breath to stay even.

"What did she say?"

Jennifer shook her head. "She wouldn't tell us exactly where she was or if she had a plan for returning."

"She reached out with no details?" He released the knob and stalked to the edge of the desk. How was he supposed to feel about this development? Of course, Nick wanted what was best for Remi, but he knew in his heart Brynn was meant to be the baby's mother.

"I'd left messages," Jennifer said softly, then shrugged when he gave her a quelling glance. "You know how this goes, Chief. We can't terminate parental rights until we do our best to reunite the mother and child. The state has a duty to contact the parent."

"She abandoned her baby," he reminded the social worker.

"I know." Jennifer sighed. "Brynn is close to being approved, but if Francesca returns to claim Remi within the allotted time frame, we have to try to make things work with the biological parent."

"It doesn't take a rocket scientist to see she isn't equipped to care for that baby. She should have no claim to Remi now."

"Stop. You don't mean what you're suggesting. It was clear that young woman was hurting, and we all need to support her if she wants to be a mother to her daughter. It's the right thing to do."

For a moment, he wished he could be old Nick—selfish Nick—the one who didn't care about doing the right thing. Instead, he gritted his teeth and nodded. "Why does doing the right thing sometimes feel like crap?"

"I wish I knew," the social worker murmured. "I convinced Francesca to schedule an appointment with me to discuss the future. We're supposed to meet a couple of days after Christmas when the office reopens. I encouraged her to tell me her plans over the phone or come in earlier, but she's visiting friends in Arizona and was adamant about the timing."

"So now we wait."

Jennifer nodded. "Do you want to tell Brynn?"

"Um, no." Nick shook his head. "Not at all."

"I'll call her, then."

"No."

The social worker blinked like she was having trouble understanding him. Nick knew he was taking a risk, but the fear of losing Remi would overshadow everything about Christmas for Brynn. He'd vowed to make her holiday happy, and he was determined to see that through.

"You want to keep this from her?" Jennifer made a tsking noise like a disappointed schoolteacher. "She has a right to know. It affects her the most."

"I get that," Nick agreed. "I just want to wait until after Christmas to tell her. She and Tyler have been through so much this year. They deserve a happy holiday, and the thought of Francesca returning would cast a shadow over everything."

"It's a real possibility that she'll want another chance with her baby."

"Yes, but not a guarantee." Nick ran a hand through his hair, wishing he could come up with a better plan. A way to tell Brynn everything now without hurting her. But he couldn't, so he'd protect her the only way he knew how.

"You said she won't be back until after the holiday anyway. I'll tell Brynn then, so she can prepare for what might happen. In the meantime, I'm holding out hope for a Christmas miracle."

Jennifer closed her eyes briefly. "I don't like this, but you know Brynn better than me. If you think the news would be too hard before Christmas, then we wait. But she has to know, Nick. Not dealing with it won't make the situation go away."

"I understand. Thanks, Jen. I promise I'll fill her in on everything. You'll call if you hear anything more from Francesca?"

"Yeah." She inclined her head as she studied him. "I'm surprised at how easily you've adjusted to taking care of a baby."

"I watched *Mr. Mom* at least half a dozen times," he said with a laugh. He needed to keep the conversation light so that he wouldn't blurt out how much Remi had come to mean to him in the past couple of weeks. Brynn wasn't the only one who'd be distraught if the baby's mother returned. He'd never admit it out loud—at least not yet—but Nick had started fantasizing about the future and what it would look like if he, Brynn, Tyler and Remi became a real family. If he claimed them as his own.

It was the future he'd never expected but one that called to his heart.

"You're doing a good job," Jennifer said. "I wish all of our foster family situations went this smoothly."

He walked her to the entrance of the station and watched as she got into her dark blue sedan and drove away. The morning had started out sunny and mild, but in the past hour the wind had picked up and gray clouds were moving in. He tried not to see the changing weather as a harbinger of things to come.

Instead, he focused on the positive. Maybe the falling temperatures and overcast skies would mean snow for the valley. A white Christmas in Starlight and a happy holiday for Brynn no matter what Nick had to do to make it so.

"You're welcome to stay a couple more days. It's not a big deal and that way Tyler and Remi could wake up together on Christmas morning."

Brynn waited until Nick turned around from loading the final suitcase into her trunk, then lifted onto her toes and brushed a kiss across his mouth. "Thank you for everything," she said, splaying her hand over his chest. They were loading her car while Remi stayed inside with Nick's mom, and Tyler had gone on a quick playdate to Max's house. "As tempted as I am by your offer, it's important for Tyler to sleep in his own bed on Christmas Eve. We have a tradition with cookies for Santa and carrots for the reindeer."

"I heard reindeer like cupcakes," Nick said, one side of his mouth curving.

"Only Rudolph." She winked. "I'm going to get us settled at the house and then we'll see you later at Parker's."

He kissed her again. "I'll miss you."

"We're talking a few hours, Chief."

"Doesn't matter." He pulled her in for a hug and she wrapped her arms around his waist.

"I wonder how many of your neighbors are watching us," she murmured.

"That doesn't matter, either." He leaned back, tipping up her chin until she met his gaze. "I don't want to hide what's going on between us."

She chewed on her bottom lip. His words sent a combination of trepidation and delight spiraling through her. She didn't want to hide, either, but a part of her still didn't trust that Nick Dunlap would be truly interested in her. So much had changed from those years of unrequited love back in high school, but her heart still bore the scars of his tacit rejection.

She'd felt like she was getting her life back on track after Daniel's death. Could she risk opening her heart to Nick again? What if he hadn't changed as much as she thought? What if he hurt her and this time she didn't recover?

"You're thinking too hard," he said, tapping her forehead with one gentle finger.

"What's going on between us?" she blurted.

He looked confused. "We're together." He said the words like they were obvious.

"But what does that mean?" She narrowed her eyes. "To you."

His chest rose and fell as he drew in a long breath, then glanced at a spot over her shoulder. Maybe she shouldn't push him. Maybe she should enjoy the way he made her feel and not worry about anything more.

But Brynn had become too good at ignoring things over the years. As much as she loved—yes, loved—Nick, she was learning that loving herself was just as important. Part of that meant not settling. She wasn't willing to simply wait to see what bone he'd throw her. The new Brynn would fight for what she wanted, but first she needed to know where they stood. If a future was even a possibility.

"It means I don't want to hide. I want to take you

on dates—more than twelve—and be a part of your life, of Tyler's and Remi's lives."

"Okay," she said slowly. It wasn't exactly the grand declaration of love she might have wanted, but it was a start. "I do have some dates to make up for."

"You've already met your dozen quota," he told her proudly. "But you can tell your friends that I've got plans for more."

She released him and took a step back. "Wait." She thought back to the past couple of weeks. "The picnic, lunch dates, candlelight dinners after the kids went to bed? Those were official dates?"

Nick looked affronted. "You couldn't tell?"

The laughter bubbled up inside her, unbidden, spilling out until she was doubled over, her shoulders shaking.

"My attempts at dating are funny to you?"

"Yes," she managed between fits of laughter.

"What did you think was happening?"

She straightened, wiping tears from the corners of her eyes, and then dissolved into another fit of giggles at the way Nick was glaring at her. "I thought you were distracting me."

"Brynn." He threw up his hands. "I'm courting you."

"No one courts anyone these days," she said, still smiling at the sweet sentiment. "We've been living together, Nick. That horse kind of left the barn already."

He shook his head. "Then it's a good thing you're moving back to your own house, because we're courting. I'm going to take you out on dates and show you off to the whole town. Heck, I might even post a selfie of the two of us to the official Facebook page." He stepped closer, cupped her cheeks between his warm palms.

The way he held her face made her feel special, cherished. And she realized that's what he'd been doing the past several weeks. No wonder she'd fallen for him all over again. He might not be the gregarious charmer of their teenage years, but his appeal as a grown man was even more devastating.

At least for her.

"You mean the world to me," he said, and her heart thumped against her chest. "I missed my chance ten years ago, but I'm going to make up for lost time."

"I like the sound of that," she said softly but pulled away when he would have kissed her again. "Right now, though, I need to unload the car before Max's mom drops off Tyler. This might be the last year he believes in Santa. I need to hide the presents while I still have time."

"Are you sure I can't pick you up tonight?" He held her hand as she moved around the car to the driver's-side door, then lifted her fingers for a soft kiss.

"I told Mara I'd get there early to help with dinner preparations. We'll see you and Remi later. Tell Ella we expect to see her there, as well."

He seemed reluctant to let her go, which made butterflies flit across her stomach all over again.

She waved in the rearview mirror and smiled at the thought that she was about to have her best Christmas ever.

"Tyler, we're leaving in ten minutes," Brynn called up the stairs a few hours later.

"I'm almost done arranging Legos," he shouted from his bedroom.

Happiness bloomed in her chest at how elated he sounded. Although she already missed being under the same roof with Nick and Remi, it was good to be back in her own house.

Her house…only better. Josh and his crew had done an amazing job with the renovation. The carpet and tile were both new, and he'd managed to find maple cabinets at a great price, so the insurance money covered all of the updates.

The first floor had received a new coat of paint, a cheery sage green that Daniel would have hated. She pressed a hand to her stomach as she thought about her late husband and the years they'd muddled along together, neither one of them anywhere near happy in their marriage.

Brynn had been so determined not to raise her

son on her own. All of her life, she'd watched and listened to her mother's subtle and obvious complaints about single parenthood. Although Brynn had never known any different, her mom seemed to believe their lives would have been so much better if Brynn's father hadn't left when she was a baby.

Her mom had always told her fatherhood was too much for some men and had encouraged her to make sure Daniel didn't see Tyler as a burden.

The implication, of course, being that Brynn had been exactly that to the man who'd left both her and her mom.

She wondered what would have happened if she or Daniel had voiced their dissatisfaction with their marriage. Obviously, her late husband found outlets for his unhappiness. Brynn had thrown herself into being the perfect mom and the most upbeat, helpful version of herself that she could.

She'd never complained. Never asked for anything for herself. Mainly because she didn't want her son to feel the guilt she'd grown up with—guilt for being born and changing her own mother's life.

But she'd been a shadow of a person and had come to not like or respect herself very much. And if she didn't respect herself, how could she expect anyone else to?

That was changing. She'd changed, and she liked the new version of herself.

She walked toward the kitchen to pull the potato

and-fennel gratin she'd made from the oven. Mara was the best baker Brynn had ever met, so they left the fancy desserts to her and the rest of the group was bringing side dishes for the meat Parker was planning to smoke. This marked the first year their group of friends was getting together for a big Christmas Eve celebration.

In the past, Daniel watched football while Brynn and Tyler binged on holiday movies in the bedroom. She'd always envied close-knit families with boisterous celebrations. Brynn's mom had left for winter in Florida and would stay there until spring.

A sound at the back door had her glancing around. She gasped and rushed forward, her heart suddenly thumping hard against her rib cage.

"Francesca," she breathed, as she threw open the door.

The petite brunette stood outside in the cold air, her hair pulled back in a low ponytail. She wore a light jacket that wasn't nearly enough protection from the wintry wind blowing. It was almost five o'clock and shadows blanketed the backyard, which was covered with a fine dusting of snow. Not enough for sledding or snowball fights but enough that they'd have a white Christmas, which had made Tyler inordinately happy.

"Merry Christmas," the other woman said, almost shyly. "I know I shouldn't be here."

"It's fine." A cacophony of emotions clamored

through her—fear, anxiety, resentment, guilt. Brynn gave herself a mental shake and stepped back into the house. "Please come in. Come out of the cold."

Francesca frowned as if she wanted to refuse but then stepped into the house. "It smells nice in here. Like garlic."

"It's a potato casserole." Brynn smiled, although the muscles of her face felt stiff. She wanted to be kind, but panic clawed at her chest. Had Francesca returned for Remi? "Can I get you a glass of water or tea?"

"No." Francesca glanced around the kitchen. "It's not the same."

"There was a fire," Brynn answered with a grimace. "Nothing serious. Faulty lights on the Christmas tree. But we had to move out for a couple of weeks. In fact, this is our first night back in the house. My son wanted to wake up here on Christmas morning. Santa Claus and all that."

"Tyler," Francesca whispered. "Daniel spoke about him often."

Resentment made Brynn's chest tighten and she resisted the urge to curl her lip. As much as she wanted to show kindness to a woman who needed it, she didn't appreciate the reminder of Francesca's relationship with Daniel. Who knew if he really had been planning to leave Brynn for this woman standing in her kitchen once again? Knowing Daniel, he could have been playing them both.

"How's Remi?" Francesca asked, her gaze darting past Brynn.

"She's good." Brynn managed another smile. "Healthy. She rolled from her back to her tummy." She pulled the phone from her back pocket. "I have a video. Would you like to see?"

"No." The word came out on a sharp exhalation of breath. "It's not a good idea. I hadn't planned on coming here." Her fingers picked at one of the buttons on her jacket.

"I'm glad you did," Brynn told her. "We were worried about you. How have you been?"

More fidgeting. "I'm staying with my cousin in Arizona, and I've been offered a job in one of the local school districts. I know the official meeting with the social worker isn't until after Christmas, but the decision about the future and Remi—it's all I can think about."

"You have a meeting scheduled with Jennifer?" Brynn frowned.

"She said she'd talk to the police chief because he's Remi's foster parent right now." She held up her hands when Brynn gaped at her, obviously misunderstanding Brynn's reaction. "I'm sure you'll be approved. Daniel told me all you cared about was being a mom. He said you probably wouldn't even notice when he left."

Brynn had trouble processing Francesca's words

over the pounding in her head. "Nick knew you were coming back?" she whispered, her voice hoarse.

"That's what the caseworker told me. But don't worry. I'm going to sign the papers to terminate my parental rights." Her voice cracked on the last words. "I want what's best for my baby, and I believe you're it. I've had a lot of time to think over the past few weeks." She laughed softly. "I've done very little except think. Can I admit something to you?"

Brynn nodded, still trying to wrap her mind around this latest turn of events.

"I didn't miss her." Francesca swiped at her cheeks and Brynn's heart ached for the pain in the woman's voice. "Does that make me a horrible person? I'm her mom, and I didn't miss her. I liked being able to sleep in and only worry about my schedule. I love her, but I don't want to be her mother."

"That's not horrible." Brynn reached out and squeezed Francesca's trembling hand. "It takes courage to do what's right for your child even when society makes you think you're wrong for that decision. I know what it's like to be judged, and I believe you're doing the right thing. I promise Remi will always know you loved her. Your daughter will grow up understanding both of her mothers loved her in the best way they could."

"Thank you," Francesca said with a sniff. "I want to tell you how sorry I am again that I believed the things Daniel said about you. That you were weak and boring. He didn't know you at all."

Brynn offered the other woman a shaky smile. "Apparently, he's not the only one. Would you like me to be there when you meet with Jennifer to sign the papers? I understand what it's like to feel alone."

"Yeah." Francesca nodded, then offered the time of the appointment. Brynn put the date into her calendar and walked Remi's biological mother to her car.

She'd offered Francesca to stay the night with them, but the woman seemed eager to be on her way.

Relief should be her overwhelming sensation. She knew that. Her mind understood it and her heart felt it, but the joy at knowing Remi would be hers was tempered by the disappointment and humiliation that Nick had kept the knowledge of Francesca's return from her.

He'd talked a good game about believing she was strong and able to handle anything, but when it mattered, he'd hidden something from her because he obviously hadn't thought she could handle it.

Like everyone else who mattered, he didn't believe in her. The question was, what was she willing to do to prove she believed in herself?

Chapter Sixteen

It was nearly ten o'clock when Nick knocked on Brynn's back door. Worry clawed at him and had been since he'd arrived at Parker and Mara's house only to be told Brynn wasn't feeling well so had decided to skip the big Christmas Eve dinner.

He'd texted her and called but gotten no response. Both Mara and Kaitlin had been acting strange, although they'd assured him that Brynn needed a quiet night to rest.

It didn't make any sense because he knew how much she'd been looking forward to the evening.

His mom had accompanied him to the dinner, so he hadn't wanted to make a scene and leave midmeal. Even Ella seemed to notice how odd it was that Brynn wasn't part of the festivities. She'd pulled him aside as he was strapping Remi into her infant seat and told him she'd stop by after the party to stay with Remi so he could check on Brynn.

His first inclination had been to refuse the offer of help, not wanting to admit there was an issue. But he still hadn't received any responses to his texts and couldn't stop the feeling that something was really wrong.

The back-porch light flicked on and a moment later Brynn appeared, a glass of wine in her hand. She wore a bulky sweatshirt and leggings with her hair pulled back into a messy bun.

"Are you sick?" he asked, noticing the high color on her cheeks and the almost wild look in her eyes.

She scrunched up her nose. "I've eaten what feels like my weight in potato casserole and nearly finished a bottle of pinot grigio. I'm not sick yet, but the night it still young. Santa and I are getting our party on."

He didn't like the edge to her voice.

"I was worried when you and Tyler didn't make it to the dinner and you never responded to my texts."

"I'm not your concern," she said, and the chill in her tone made the little hairs on the back of his neck stand on end. "Despite what you seem to think, I can handle my life."

"I know you can," he agreed, trying to figure out what the hell was wrong. "Could I come in?"

She drained her glass and then shrugged. "You're going to do whatever you want anyway. Let's not pretend you care about my thoughts or feelings."

"I care." Despite her flippant attitude, he could almost feel the pain radiating from her. He didn't understand it, but it sliced across his heart like a razor. "Brynn, what the hell is the problem?"

"No problem. In fact, I'm celebrating. Making spirits bright and all that." Without warning, she turned and stalked toward the counter, pouring another large glass of wine for herself.

Nick followed her and closed the door to the winter air, which did nothing for the chill that settled in his chest. Something was very off with the woman he loved. He knew how hard the holidays were after the death of someone close. As troubled as their marriage had been, Daniel had been Brynn's husband for a decade. It was a lot of time to spend with a person. A lot of making Christmas joyous for their son. She'd been so strong these past few weeks— months, even—maybe the pressure had finally become too much for her.

What would it take for her to reach out and let him support her? How could he prove he was a man she could depend on?

"I love you," he blurted out, watching as if in slow motion as she whirled toward him, her eyes wide with shock and something that looked like rage. No, he had to be mistaken. Rage didn't make a bit of sense.

Wine sloshed over the side of her glass, and she placed it on the counter, then stalked toward him, finger wagging. "Don't say that to me. Don't you dare."

"It's true," he whispered, palms up like he could diffuse her anger somehow. "Brynn, please. Tell me what's wrong. I can't stand to see you like this."

"Francesca came to see me today."

Nick blinked. "No. She's not supposed to be in town until…"

The words tapered off when Brynn's gaze narrowed. "I wanted you to enjoy Christmas without worrying about losing Remi," he said, not bothering to pretend he no longer understood her anger. "I was trying to protect you. Don't be mad."

"I can feel however I want to feel," she said, enunciating each word. "I'm not a delicate flower, Nick. I don't need to be sheltered. I won't fall apart at the first hint of something difficult. Do you know how many difficult things I've dealt with over the years?"

"Yes." He nodded. "I do, and I know you can handle anything."

"But you didn't trust me to handle the idea of losing Remi."

"I was going to tell you after Christmas. We don't even know exactly what she's thinking."

"I know," Brynn said through clenched teeth. "I know because my late husband's mistress is the only person who seems to think I can manage the truth. My own mother didn't think I could handle becoming a mom and taking care of a baby. Daniel was afraid to leave me because he thought I'd fall apart." She laughed. "Heck, even my friends don't trust that I can find a man on my own, so they have to concoct some sort of dating game for me. And you're the worst of the lot."

His heart twisted at the accusation. "I promise I was trying to protect you. Nothing more."

"I thought you understood I don't need protection. I need someone to believe in me, to support me in standing on my own two feet. I want a partner, not a protector."

Nick ran a hand over his face, took a step toward her, then stopped when she crossed her arms over her chest. "Brynn, I failed you in high school. I failed my brother and my family. I was selfish and self-centered. This is me trying to do the right thing."

"It's you trying to control every aspect of the situation because you're afraid of what might happen if you don't," she countered.

Yes. Yes, he wanted control. He'd purposely shirked responsibility for most of his youth, and in doing so had hurt the people he loved. Brynn most of all.

"I didn't want you to be hurt."

"You need to learn that I can handle being hurt, Nick." She shook her head. "I'm practically a damn expert at it."

"Does she want to be reunited with the baby?" he asked quietly. "Why did she come to see you and not me?"

She stared at him for several long moments and then answered, "Nick, I fell in love with you before I even understood what love was. But I know now. I know what I want from love. It's more than having someone take care of me. I need a man who will be at my side to support me taking care of myself, as well. Someone who will trust me with their weaknesses and fears as much as I trust them."

She pressed a hand to her stomach. "For years, I made myself small because it's what I thought was the right thing to have a happy marriage. But neither one of us was the least bit happy. I owe it to my son and my soon-to-be daughter to be a role model."

"You are a role model to so many people," he agreed.

Her gaze had gone from angry to sad, which scared him even more. "I thought we might have another chance, but I can't be with a man who doesn't believe in me."

"I do, Brynn. So much."

"No. There's a difference between caring and coddling." She reached out a hand and gripped the edge of the counter with her fingers like she needed the support. "I think you should go now," she said without the barest hint of emotion in her voice.

He wanted to rail and argue. This wasn't how it was supposed to go. Tonight was Christmas Eve. He'd planned to spend the evening celebrating with their friends and then tomorrow morning enjoy the holiday together as a family.

But once again, he'd failed someone he loved. It didn't matter that his own heart was breaking in the process. He knew he wasn't cut out for relationships. Hell, he had a string of ex-girlfriends who could attest to that.

Tears shone in Brynn's blue eyes, and he hated himself for putting them there. He hadn't trusted her. He was afraid without Remi to bind them she'd realize she deserved better than he could give her. He'd lied to her for reasons he thought were valid, but he'd been a coward. Now he had to deal with the consequences.

"I'm sorry," he said, and the words had never sounded lamer.

She gave a tight nod. "Me, too."

It felt like slogging through mud, but he forced himself to turn around and walk away, knowing he was leaving behind his best chance at happiness.

* * *

"The Roman Colosseum," Tyler shouted, as he held up the box for his mom to see. "Can I put it together now, Mom?"

"Sure, sweetie." Brynn bounced Remi on her knee and tried to make her smile seem normal.

"Should I wait for Nick to come over so he can help?"

The innocent question was like a dagger to her heart.

Ella set a plate of cookies on the coffee table. "Nick ended up having to work today, bud. Official police chief business. I'm sure he'd want you to go ahead with the Lego set."

Tyler snagged a cookie and nodded. "Maybe he'll come by when he gets off. Mom, can I use your phone to FaceTime Max? I want to see what he got for Christmas and then I'll start."

"Five minutes, Ty." She handed him the phone, and he grabbed the gifts he'd just opened, kissed Remi's cheek and headed upstairs to his room.

"Thank you," Brynn said to Ella when they were alone with Remi. "I'm going to have to get better at answering questions about Nick. It's funny because I'm so used to talking about Daniel with Tyler. Now to have another man disappear from his life…" She swallowed back a sob. "It's too much, you know?"

Ella sat down on the chair across from Brynn and broke off a bite of cookie. It was a few minutes past noon on Christmas, and Brynn had expected to have a quiet day with Tyler until Ella texted and told her she was bringing over Remi for a visit.

Apparently, Nick had asked his temporary nanny to bring Remi for a holiday visit with Brynn and Tyler. It made her so happy to hold the sweet baby, although she could faintly make out Nick's scent when she snuggled the girl to her chest. The wave of longing that rose inside her threatened to take her under.

"He's still there," Ella said softly. "It's none of my business, but the guy is beside himself broken up about what happened."

"It wasn't just that something happened." Brynn shook her head. "He lied to me. He didn't trust me to handle the truth."

Ella sighed. "I have control issues, too. Blame it on my job or all the years of living out of a suitcase."

"I haven't left Starlight beyond a couple of weeks of vacation for over a decade," Brynn told her. "What's my excuse?"

"You don't need an excuse, but you might want to think about giving Nick another chance."

"I don't even know that he wants one. Our deal was not for anything long-term. We both knew it would end when Remi came to live with me."

Her brain might have been muddled last night by the wine, but one thing stayed clear. She and Nick had been a temporary thing. If he'd really known her, he would have trusted her with the truth of Francesca's upcoming visit.

"Did you, though?"

Brynn lifted Remi above her head and kissed the tip of the baby's nose when she giggled. "I'm a mom. That's my deal."

Ella rolled her eyes. "News flash. Women who are mothers are also human. You're allowed to have needs beyond your kids."

"Easy for you to say."

"Doesn't make it less true." Ella leaned forward and pushed the plate of cookies toward Brynn. "You need a cookie and you need a man. Nick specifically."

"I need a bunch of cookies." Brynn plucked one from the tray. "And a decent night's sleep and a million dollars and fresh highlights in my hair." She took a big bite and said around a mouthful of chocolate-chip goodness, "But not a man."

Ella laughed. "Not convincing at all."

Remi let out a wide yawn. "You should take her back to Nick's," Brynn said as emotion welled up inside her. "She's getting tired."

"I'm sorry for all of this." Ella watched with sympathetic eyes as Brynn lowered Remi into the infant seat and fastened the straps.

"None of it is your fault." Brynn swiped at her cheeks. "I have so much to be happy about and crying on Christmas is ridiculous."

"I won't judge you for being ridiculous." Ella winked. "But for the love of everything holy, enough with the waterworks."

Brynn gasped, and Ella gave her shoulder a gentle nudge. "Just kidding, but I snapped you out of the crying, right?"

"Actually, yes." Brynn had never met anyone like Ella Samuelson. She appreciated how the woman had assumed the role of friend without hesitation. Brynn had a habit of second-guessing every minute detail of her life. The relationship with Nick being a prime example.

But before she could deal with him, she had to get the rest of her emotional life in order. Tyler and Remi deserved that.

"I almost forgot." Ella slipped an envelope out of her purse as she hooked the infant seat over her arm. "Nick asked me to give this to you. He said it's a copy of the letter he submitted to social services."

Brynn frowned. "About me?"

"I guess they asked him for a reference letter. I don't know if it's because you two are friends or in his capacity as police chief. It's still strange that never-serious Nick is the law around here now, you know?"

"Yeah," Brynn breathed, her fingers numb as she took the envelope from Ella.

She gave Remi a last snuggle and then walked them to Ella's Jeep. After they drove away, she checked on Tyler, who was engrossed in his latest Lego set. With nothing else to act as a distraction, she sat down on the edge of her bed, holding the letter between two fingers. Her heart pounded as she contemplated whether to even open it.

Did she want to see what Nick had written about her? Did it matter?

"Stop pretending," she muttered to herself after a few moments. It mattered. She ripped open the seal and began to read.

Chapter Seventeen

"She's yours." Kaitlin smoothed a finger over Remi's soft hair and grinned at Brynn. "For always."

"Not yet." Brynn held up a hand. "Don't jinx it. I have at least a couple more months until the adoption is finalized."

"But she's here." Mara joined them as they stood behind the kitchen island, looking out to the friends who had gathered in Brynn's renovated kitchen and family room.

The party to celebrate Remi becoming her official foster daughter, along with the New Year, had been Kaitlin's idea. Although Brynn often wasn't comfortable being the center of attention, she'd agreed.

She wanted to celebrate this milestone. She was choosing to become the baby's mother and she didn't care what anyone else thought of her decision. It was so different than how she'd felt as a pregnant high school graduate, embarrassed and frightened about what the future might hold.

"How's Nick?" she asked suddenly, unable to keep her curiosity at bay one moment longer.

Both of her friends focused on the baby.

"Come on," she urged. "I'm going to see him eventually, and I know Finn and Parker have been talking to him. I still care about him even if it didn't work out between us. Again."

"You know he really does love you?" Kaitlin glanced from Remi to Brynn.

She met her friend's concerned gaze. "I think he wanted to love me," she answered, allowing Kaitlin to take the baby from her arms. "But not in the way I want to be loved. I'm not the timid girl I used to be," she said, more to herself than her friends. "I thought Nick and I could make a fresh start, but maybe there's too much past between us. Maybe he's still trying to make up for setting me up with Daniel."

"That was an unfortunate move," Mara said with a small laugh.

"But the choice to go out with Daniel and sleep with him and to marry him after I ended up pregnant were mine. I spent a long time making excuses for not taking responsibility in my life. Things happened to me," Brynn said, sighing, "but I let them. I controlled my reaction."

Kaitlin arched a brow. "And now you've cut Nick out of your life to prove you're in control."

Brynn let out a gasp of surprise. "That makes me sound foolish and petty."

Kaitlin feigned surprise. "Does it now?"

"And you're an expert on relationships?" Brynn asked.

"Before Finn, I was an expert on screwing up relationships," Kaitlin clarified. "My baggage had baggage, but I can still see when two people were meant for each other. Everyone can see what's between you."

"It's true," Mara confirmed.

Brynn sighed and turned to the counter to refill her coffee mug. "I gave up everything to make a go at marriage with a man I didn't love. I thought it was the right thing to do. I'm finally coming into my own, but it's not going to work if I'm with a man who tries to shelter me from anything bad. I want someone who will walk through fire with me, not for me."

"Oh, honey." Mara placed a hand on Brynn's arm. "Trust me, you want both."

Brynn blinked as her brain scrambled for purchase with that thought taking hold. Maybe she'd gone too far with her need to stand on her own two feet. Too many years of being brushed aside or underestimated had definitely made the pendulum swing in the other direction when it came to her desire to feel independent and in control.

"It's too late now," she whispered.

"He's miserable," Mara blurted out, then threw up her hands when Kaitlin gave her a quelling look. "What? It's true."

"We weren't supposed to say that out loud." Kaitlin turned to Brynn, shifting Remi in her arms as she did. "This hasn't been easy for Nick, either. To everyone's surprise—including his own, I imagine—he liked having a baby in the house. And you and Tyler, too, of course. But he wants you to be happy."

"We all do," Mara added.

"He's going to give you the time and distance you need, and he's telling Finn and Parker that all he wants is to be your friend again if you'll give him a chance."

"Do you think that's true?" Brynn drew in a shaky breath.

"I think you need to decide what you want from him and then be brave enough to ask for it." Kaitlin dropped a kiss on the top of Remi's head, then smiled. "To get what you want, sometimes you have to risk being hurt."

"I'm not great at asking for what I want," Brynn said with a shake of her head. "I'm more the take-the-lemons-life-hands-me-and-try-to-make-a-whole-meal-out-of-them type of person."

"Remember—" Mara leaned in "—this is new Brynn. Brynn 2.0."

Brynn held up a hand. "Fine. But no more talk about a dozen dates. I'm done with playing games, even well-intentioned ones."

"I thought you'd been on your twelve dates," Kaitlin said softly.

With Nick. A slow ache expanded in Brynn's chest but before she could respond to her friend, Tyler came running up to her. "Mom, you need to get Evie and Anna out of my room. They keep trying to touch my Lego sets. Anna wants to turn the fire station into a beauty salon." He threw up his hands in obvious disgust. "Like where girls get their hair cut."

Remi began to cry.

"She's probably hungry," Brynn said to Kaitlin. "Let me take her."

"Mom, you've got to make them leave." Tyler crossed his arms over his thin chest. "I want everyone to leave."

"Ty, be nice." Brynn bounced Remi in an attempt to quiet her, but the baby was having none of it. She smiled as several guests looked over toward them, familiar embarrassment causing heat to creep along the back of her neck. She didn't need a baby and a boy meltdown at the moment. "Everyone is here to celebrate your sister."

"I'll handle the girls," Mara said, reaching out to pat Tyler's shoulder. He yanked away with narrowed eyes.

"They're stupid," he muttered.

"Tyler." Frustration made Brynn's tone sharper than she'd meant.

"It's fine." Mara headed for the stairs with Tyler stalking after her.

"I think it's also time for the celebration to wrap up," Kaitlin said.

Remi's cries grew louder. "I need to get her fed." Brynn took a premixed bottle of formula from the refrigerator and popped it into the bottle warmer Ella had brought over along with the other supplies from Nick's house.

"Don't worry about any of us," Kaitlin told her.

But Brynn did worry. Once the bottle heated, she moved to the kitchen table and sat down with Remi. The baby sucked hungrily but remained uncharacteristically fussy. Her friends cleaned up the food and paper products, talking in hushed tones as if that would help Remi feel better.

Maybe it would. Maybe, like Brynn, the baby was overwhelmed. Mara reappeared with Anna and Evie, both looking irritated, and threw Brynn an apologetic glance.

Parker and Josh hustled the girls out of the house,

and Mara walked toward the table. "Evie accidentally knocked down one of the completed sets. I helped gather as many of the scattered bricks as I could find, but Tyler's pretty upset."

"Thank you. He'll be fine. I'll check on him as soon as Remi finishes."

She accepted hugs from both Mara and Kaitlin, and after another round of thanking them for their help and support, her friends left.

Brynn blinked away tears. Not because she was overwhelmed at this moment. She'd had plenty of struggles as a mom and knew she could deal with cranky babies and angry ten-year-olds. But she couldn't help but wonder if she'd done the right thing for all of them. Tyler, Remi and her. Was this new normal—the bumpy road of being a single mother to two children—the best future she could offer?

She couldn't imagine loving another man besides Nick, and now she'd pushed him away because of her anger and pride. What kind of example did that set for her children?

Remi continued to fuss as Brynn patted the baby's back to elicit a burp. After she'd taken the bottle, Brynn headed upstairs with the girl still crying. A nap was definitely in order, maybe for all of them at this point.

She knocked on Tyler's door and was greeted with a firm, "Go away."

"I'm sorry about your Legos," she said through the door. "Do you want help?"

"I want Remi to be quiet," he shouted back.

"Working on that, bud," she told him. "I'm going to put her down for a nap and then we can spend some time together."

She took his silence for agreement and turned on the night-light and sound machine in Remi's bedroom. The room was small and still held the bed and dresser from its previous use as a guest bedroom.

Brynn changed the baby's diaper while Remi fussed and then sang her several lullabies before placing her on her back on the gingham sheet.

Remi continued to wail, so Brynn lay down on the bed, planning to watch the baby for a few minutes until she settled. She had a feeling Remi was simply overstimulated after so much attention at the party. Since it was out of character for the little one to cry this way, Brynn didn't want to take any chances.

Once she made sure Remi was okay, she needed to spend some quality time with Tyler. He'd been a trouper with all the changes, but she knew this transition would have a few bumps, and she needed to take care of her first baby as well as the new one.

"Your mom is going to be really worried," Nick said, glancing into the rearview mirror as he drove the short distance between his house and Brynn's.

"All she cares about is Remi," Tyler muttered. He used one finger to draw patterns on the misty window. "It's exactly what Max said would happen. I hate Remi." The last three words came out on a choked sob, and Nick immediately pulled over and shifted the car into Park.

He undid his seat belt and turned to face Tyler, who looked as miserable as a grubby-faced boy could manage. Tyler had shown up at Nick's house on his bicycle, winded and spewing a convoluted story about how Mara's and Josh's respective daughters ruined his most recently completed Lego set, the one Nick had given him for Christmas. He hated girls and he hated his new sister and he wanted to come and live with Nick where there were no females in the house.

The boy had been brimming with frustration, and it took Nick a full five minutes to understand that Tyler had left the house without telling his mom where he was going. Nick had tried calling and texting Brynn but had gotten no answer. Once Tyler calmed down, Nick explained they had to return to his mom's house so she wouldn't panic when she realized he was gone.

"Is that true?" Nick asked gently.

The kid's jaw worked for several seconds before he gave a sharp shake of his head. "No, but it's her fault that Evie broke my Lego set. And Mom loves Remi better than me now."

"I know that's not true." Nick's heart melted for the boy. Tyler had been a pint-size emotional rock during these past few weeks and in the months after his father's death. Nick knew it couldn't be easy to deal with all of the changes, especially when Tyler obviously felt like he had to be strong for his mom. "She loves you more than anything in the world, and she has since the day you were born. Even before. I was the first person she told she was having a baby."

"Even before my dad?" Tyler's feathery brows drew together.

"Your mom was my best friend back in high school," Nick said instead of answering the question directly. "We told each other everything. She was nervous like young mothers are, but I could see in her eyes how happy the thought of you made her. I knew she'd be an amazing mom."

"I don't want to hate Remi," Tyler said. "I want her to be my sister, but I'm so mad."

"You're allowed to be mad at your sister," Nick assured him.

"But she's a baby."

"I know." Nick smiled. "It's still okay. It doesn't mean you don't love her. You do."

The boy drew in a shaky breath. "Yeah."

"I guarantee she'll make you mad about a million more times in your life, but you'll still love her. That's how it is with brothers and sisters."

"Do you have a sister?"

"No." Nick shook his head. "I had a brother, but he died. I miss him every day. He was a way nicer person than I am."

"You're nice to me," Tyler told him with a sniff. "And to Mom. Are you guys still friends?"

"I'll always be your mom's friend. She needed some time to adjust to the changes when Remi came to live with you, so I probably won't get to see you as much now. Babies take a lot of attention, but she still loves you as much as she did before."

"You and I can still hang out, right?"

Pain sliced across Nick's chest at the expectation in the boy's gaze.

"I hope so," he whispered, then turned back around and fastened his seat belt. "Right now, we need get you home."

A profusion of thoughts cascaded through his mind as he turned onto Brynn's street. He'd hated everything about the past week and blamed himself for making her believe he didn't have faith in her. If he'd only told the damn truth in the first place, maybe they wouldn't be here right now.

Or maybe they would. He still struggled to believe he could be the man Brynn deserved. But damn if he wasn't going to give it his best shot. Not just because he loved her, though he knew no one would ever have the hold on his heart that she did. It was more than just their connection. He loved Tyler and Remi and the thought of the three of them becoming his family made a peace descend over him that felt like coming home.

Now he needed to convince Brynn he could be her home, as well.

His phone beeped as he parked in her driveway. "Brynn?"

"Oh, my God, Nick." He hated the panic in her voice. "Do you have him? Tell me you have him. I fell asleep and—"

"We're here, Brynn. He's home." He turned off the engine.

She made a noise somewhere between a sob and a cheer and he heard a sound like she'd dropped the phone to the floor.

Tyler was already climbing out of the back seat and looked over his shoulder. He flashed a sheepish grin. "I guess you were right. She missed me."

Nick didn't have time to answer before they both turned when Brynn shouted for her son. Nick's chest tightened as he watched Brynn tear across the front lawn and scoop Tyler into her arms, hugging him tight until the boy squirmed.

"You're squishing me," the boy complained.

"You scared me half to death." Brynn drew back, holding Tyler's thin arms. "I couldn't find you, sweetie. I didn't know what to think. Please don't ever leave without telling me."

"You were asleep," he said, and she frowned at the soft admonishment in his tone.

"I'm sorry, Ty. But you can wake me. Please. I always have time for you."

"Don't cry." The boy wiped her cheeks with the sleeve of his striped sweater. "I was mad. Nick hadn't been over to see the Colosseum since I finished it, and I wanted to tell him."

"I'm glad you had a friend to go to." She bit down on her lower lip as she offered Nick a watery smile.

"He told me you love me best of all," Tyler said.

Brynn's gaze filled with gratitude before she returned her attention to her son, and Nick felt his heart stammer in response.

"I will always love you with my whole heart," she told her son, giving him another hug.

"But now you love Remi, too." Tyler pulled away.

"There's room in my heart for both of you," she promised. "When Remi came into our lives, Ty, my heart grew with love. So much."

Nick stepped closer as the boy seemed to mull this over. "I guess that makes sense. But she's annoying when she cries."

"There will be plenty of things your sister does over the years that annoy you."

"Nick told me that, too." Tyler nodded. "He said I'll love her anyway."

"Yeah," Brynn whispered.

"Mom, can Nick come in and help me start putting the Colosseum back together?"

The way Brynn frowned made Nick's stomach

clench. *Please don't say no*, he thought. "If he has time, it's okay with me."

They both turned their attention to Nick, and he nodded, trying not to look like a lovesick puppy.

"Maybe you can stay for dinner so you can visit with Remi, too?" Brynn straightened and a blush crept up her cheeks. "If you aren't too busy?"

"I'd love that," he said, grateful when he managed to get the words out with a steady voice.

Tyler grinned, then tugged on his mom's hand. "Let's go."

"You head in," she told him and dropped a kiss on the top of his head. "Nick and I will be there in a minute."

"I'll bring everything downstairs," he told Nick, then looked toward his mom. "And I'll be quiet, so I don't wake Remi."

"Thanks, sweetie."

They both watched him walk away, and an awkward silence descended between them. Nick hated the damn silence. This was Brynn. His best friend. The love of his life, even if it had taken him far too long to realize it.

"I'm sorry," he said at the same time as her.

His eyes widened as she offered a small smile. "Jinx," she murmured.

"Brynn, no." His hands itched to reach for her, but he wouldn't yet. If he touched her, he'd lose all ability for coherent thought and this part was important. "You have nothing to apologize for. I'm sorry I didn't tell you about Francesca. It was stupid and selfish, which should come as no surprise from me."

"You aren't stupid or selfish."

"Always so kind."

"Not always," she reminded him.

He nodded. "You were right to call me out on what I did, but I need you to know I have all the faith in the world in you. Just not in myself. Or in the fact that you would actually choose me if there was nothing to keep us apart."

"Nick." She took a step closer.

He lifted his hand, then ran it through his hair instead of pulling her to him. "I can't promise I won't keep screwing up, Brynn. I'll probably be annoying and stupid and a huge idiot for the rest of my life."

She chuckled. "Is this the part where you're pumping yourself up?"

He dropped down to one knee. "This is the part where I ask you to love me anyway."

Her mouth formed a small o.

"Please give me another chance and I promise I won't waste it. Brynn, I want to spend the rest of our lives trying to do better. Trying to be the kind of man that deserves you."

"Silly," she whispered and cupped his face with her palms. The warmth and softness of her skin against his made his whole body tingle with longing. "It's always been you, Nick. I will always choose you. I pushed you away because I was scared, not because I can't handle mistakes or missteps. We're both going to make those. But I want to make them together."

It felt like a firework display erupted in his heart, and he could lose himself in the bright intensity of it. "Will you marry me, Brynn Hale? Will you make me the happiest man in the world?"

She leaned in and whispered against his lips, "Yes."

And Nick knew, with every ounce of his being, that he'd truly found his home.

* * * * *

Don't miss Michelle Major's next book,
Her Texas New Year's Wish,
the first book in
The Fortunes of Texas: The Hotel Fortune
miniseries,
coming January 2021 from
Harlequin Special Edition!

And don't miss any of these other
great holiday romances:

A Soldier Under Her Tree
by Kathy Douglass

A Firehouse Christmas Baby
by Teri Wilson

A Sheriff's Star
by Makenna Lee

Available now wherever Harlequin Special Edition
books and ebooks are sold!

When Grace Williams topples from the balcony at the new Hotel Fortune, the last thing she expects is to find love with her new bosses' brother. Wiley Fortune has looks, money and charm to spare. But Grace's past makes her wary of investing her heart. This time, she is holding out for the real deal…

Read on for a sneak peek at
Her Texas New Year's Wish
by Michelle Major, the first book in
The Fortunes of Texas: The Hotel Fortune!

"I didn't fall," she announced with a wide smile as he returned the crutches.

"You did great." He looked at her with a huge smile.

"That was silly," she said as they started down the walk toward his car. "Maneuvering down a few steps isn't a big deal, but this is the farthest I've gone on my own since the accident. If my parents had their way, they'd encase me in Bubble Wrap for the rest of my life to make sure I stayed safe."

"It's an understandable sentiment from people who care about you."

"But not what I want."

He opened the car door for her, and she gave him the crutches to stow in the back seat. The whole process was slow and awkward. By the time Grace was buckled in next to Wiley, sweat dripped between her shoulder blades, and she felt like she'd run a marathon. How could less than a week of inactivity make her feel like such an invalid?

As if sensing her frustration, Wiley placed a gentle hand on her arm. "You've been through a lot, Grace. Your ankle and the cast are the biggest outward signs of the accident, but you fell from the second story."

She offered a wan smile. "I have the bruises to prove it."

"Give yourself a bit of…well, grace."

"I never thought of attorneys as naturally comforting people," she admitted. "But you're good at giving support."

"It's a hidden skill." He released her hand and pulled away from the curb. "We lawyers don't like to let anyone know about our human side. It ruins the reputation of being coldhearted, and then people aren't afraid of us."

"You're the opposite of scary."

"Where are we headed?" he asked when he got to the stop sign at the end of the block.

"The highway," she said without hesitation. "As much as I love Rambling Rose, I need a break. Let's get out of this town, Wiley."

Get 4 FREE REWARDS!

We'll send you 2 FREE Books
<u>plus</u> 2 FREE Mystery Gifts.

Harlequin Special Edition books relate to finding comfort and strength in the support of loved ones and enjoying the journey no matter what life throws your way.

FREE
Value Over
$20

IF YOU ENJOYED THIS BOOK
WE THINK YOU WILL ALSO LOVE

LOVE INSPIRED

INSPIRATIONAL ROMANCE

Uplifting stories of faith, forgiveness and hope.

Fall in love with stories where faith helps
guide you through life's challenges, and discover
the promise of a new beginning.

6 NEW BOOKS AVAILABLE EVERY MONTH!

SPECIAL EXCERPT FROM

LOVE INSPIRED
INSPIRATIONAL ROMANCE

When a city slicker wants the same piece of land
as a small-town girl, will sparks fly between them?

Read on for a sneak preview of
Opening Her Heart
by Deb Kastner.

What on earth?

Suddenly, a shiny red Mustang came around the curve of the driveway at a speed far too fast for the dirt road, and when the vehicle slammed to a stop, it nearly hit the side of Avery's SUV.

Who drove that way, especially on unpaved mountain roads?

The man unfolded himself from the driver's seat and stood to his full over-six-foot height, let out a whoop of pure pleasure and waved his black cowboy hat in the air before combing his fingers through his thick dark hair and settling the hat on his head.

Avery had never seen him before in her life.

It wasn't so much that they didn't have strangers occasionally visiting Whispering Pines. Avery's own family brought in customers from all over Colorado who wanted the full Christmas tree–cutting experience.

So, yes, there were often strangers in town.

But this man?

He was as out of place as a blue spruce in an orange grove. And he was on land she intended to purchase—before anyone else was supposed to know about it.

Yes, he sported a cowboy hat and boots similar to those that the men around the Pines wore, but his whole getup probably cost more than Avery made in a year, and his new boots gleamed from a fresh polish.

Avery fought to withhold a grin, thinking about how quickly those shiny boots would lose their luster with all the dirt he'd raised with his foolish driving.

Served him right.

Just what was this stranger doing *here*?

"And didn't you say the cabin wasn't listed yet?" Avery said quietly. "What does this guy think he's doing here?"

"I have no idea how—" Lisa whispered back.

"Good afternoon, ladies," said the man as he tipped his hat, accompanied by a sparkle in his deep blue eyes and a grin Avery could only categorize as charismatic. He could easily have starred in a toothpaste commercial.

She had a bad feeling about this.

As the man approached, the puppy at Avery's heels started barking and straining against his lead—something he'd been in training not to do. Was he trying to protect her, to tell her this man was bad news?

Don't miss
Opening Her Heart *by Deb Kastner,*
available January 2021 wherever
Love Inspired *books and ebooks are sold.*

LoveInspired.com